T0207667

QUESTS

QUESTS

JOHN M. BREWER

QUESTS

This is a work of fiction. All of the characters, names, incidents,
organizations, and dialogue in this novel are either the products
of the author's imagination or are used fictitiously.

iUniverse books may be ordered through booksellers or by contacting:

iUniverse
1663 Liberty Drive
Bloomington, IN 47403
www.iuniverse.com
1-800-Authors (1-800-288-4677)

Because of the dynamic nature of the Internet, any web addresses or
links contained in this book may have changed since publication and
may no longer be valid. The views expressed in this work are solely those
of the author and do not necessarily reflect the views of the publisher,
and the publisher hereby disclaims any responsibility for them.

Any people depicted in stock imagery provided by Thinkstock are
models, and such images are being used for illustrative purposes only.
Certain stock imagery © Thinkstock.

ISBN: 978-1-5320-0925-9 (sc)
ISBN: 978-1-5320-0924-2 (e)

Library of Congress Control Number: 2016918193

Print information available on the last page.

iUniverse rev. date: 11/04/2016

"To my wife
From my most successful quest"

NEGOTIATIONS

The tall woman with iron-gray hair in charge of the Winnemucca Museum had put on her stone-wall face, but Joe Stallings was expecting it. He waited for her to give her reasons. He was fairly confident because he had what he hoped was a clinching argument.

"The Native American Burial Act forbids taking samples for studies like the one you propose," she said.

Joe replied, "The legends of the local Native Americans, the Paiutes, clearly consider these people to not be of their tribe or of any tribe known to them. The Paiutes massacred all of them, so the Paiutes aren't going to object. And their descriptions are clear and consistent: very tall, with red hair. So the remains you have are not from Native Americans. What I propose to do is take a sample of bone, analyze its DNA, and show they came from somewhere else.

"Now," Joe continued, "I may be able to show conclusively the ancestry or ethnicity of the remains you have but possibly also whether the person whose skull you showed me had red hair, what eye color he or she had, maybe even some other traits associated with European ancestry, such as lactase persistence.

And if, as the odds favor, the skull is from someone of European ethnicity, the Native American Burial Act is just irrelevant.

"Plus," Joe went on, "consider the publicity. You—this museum—will be swamped with visitors. Right now there are legends. What I can do—and will do, given a bone sample from that skull—is put legends, hearsay, and gossip on a solid scientific basis. And if I can get a big enough sample of bone or something else made of carbon, I can date when that person died."

She was wavering—Joe could see. She asked, "Can you do that sort of analysis?"

"I have done so, many times."

This was an exaggeration, but Joe had carried out such measurements on more recent samples and was confident he could do so on the skull he had seen.

He added, "If the DNA in the skull turns out to be Native American, no more will be said. But the odds are the skull is from someone of European ethnicity. And the odds are also in favor of the skull being pre-Columbian, perhaps by hundreds of years. You will have a media circus in this place."

"How much do you need?" she asked.

Joe suppressed a feeling of triumph and just answered honestly, "More sample is better. Say, a molar. I strongly doubt anyone will notice. But I will be able to get a lot of information from that—believe me. And it is better to get what information we can, now, before we have another fire."

She nodded. Many of the remains from the Lovelock Cave had been destroyed in a fire, a thought that made Joe cringe whenever he remembered it.

Joe put another nail in the coffin, so to speak. "The results will be published in a reputable scientific journal," he said.

Joe didn't add that he hoped to get his PhD in applied genetics. He wanted the woman to think he was a professional, which in a sense he was. He needed the results he hoped to get for his doctoral dissertation. And that, in turn, would open many doors.

There was another woman in the office. She had kept quiet during Joe's proposal.

Now she asked him, "When do you want to get the tooth?"

Looking at her for the first time, Joe saw she was a middle-sized, sturdy-looking younger woman with curly brown hair and brown eyes. She also had a badge with her name and job title on it, but Joe couldn't read the badge from where he was sitting.

But he answered, "Let me get my gear out of my truck, and I'll take the tooth out right away."

The older woman looked cornered but did not object. The idea of a media circus probably appealed to her. Joe figured she imagined it would keep the Humboldt County commissioners quiet, at least for a while.

Joe brought his kit in to another room, where the younger woman had brought the skull. He put on a face mask and gloves and took out a sterile bottle and a pair of vise-grip pliers. This was window dressing, since the skull had lain in bat dung, probably for centuries, and then been handled many times, but Joe hoped it would impress the women. He also took out a jar of antibacterial soap solution. He looked carefully at the jawbone of the skull to find the biggest molar he could.

The size of the teeth was impressive. Relieved to find no obvious tooth decay in most of them, he made his choice. He opened the jar of antibacterial soap, dipped the teeth of the vise grips in it for a minute or so, and then used them to pull the tooth he wanted. It came out fairly easily, and Joe put the tooth into the sterile bottle.

"Done," he said, rather unnecessarily.

"When will you have the results?" asked the older woman.

Joe said, "I will start work as soon as I get back to Reno. Perhaps a week, perhaps two."

This was a little reckless, but Joe had set everything up in his adviser's lab, and Joe was the only student, so his work there should not be disturbed. He had only the two weeks, and he figured he'd be able to meet his deadline.

"I will phone you with my results."

The older woman, however, told Joe, "Give them to Penny here. I go on vacation next week."

Joe nodded, and Penny gave Joe her card. Joe saw the younger woman's name was Penny Echeverria, and she was the assistant director.

Leaving the museum, Joe was thinking Penny rather attractive, but he had forgotten to look for a wedding ring. Anyway, now he had the tooth. He had a lot of work to do and less than two weeks to do it. He got in his truck and headed west, back to Reno.

ANCIENT HISTORY: STACEY

More years back than Joe cared to calculate, he had been a shy, awkward undergraduate at the University of Nevada. He had no social skills whatever but was a very good student, so, having decided to get a PhD in genetics, he had applied for admission to the genetics program.

He not only was admitted to candidacy in the genetics program there but was awarded a federal fellowship. His road was clear and, even better, paid for.

That summer, he worked at a DNA testing laboratory, a local branch of a company called GeneQuestion, the sort of business that establishes parentage or rules it out. Unusually, he was paid, since he had a BS. In fact, he was paid well enough to be able to pay off his school loans, which had been kept relatively modest, thanks to his scholarship. So that fall, he was feeling flush for the first time in his life. He had a bank account and a credit card, though he never used the card.

Aside from taking courses, his duties required him to be a teaching assistant (TA) in the Introductory Genetics class, which included a laboratory. There, in Joe's second year, one of his students was a very pretty woman named Stacey Porter.

Joe heard the other male students privately calling her Stacey Porterhouse, thinking of her as a superior cut of meat. Stacey had honey-blond hair—it was extensively debated whether that was its natural color—and blue eyes, but most of all a spectacular figure. This prompted more debate about her bra size, whether the bra was padded, and to what extent.

She stood about five feet six inches tall, an inch shorter than Joe.

Though Joe was a conscientious TA who tried to help all his students, he spent a disproportionate amount of time with Stacey. This was not because she needed that much more help, for she was fairly bright, but because Joe very quickly fell in love with her.

He couldn't ask her out, partly because he was too shy but also because it was made clear to all the TAs that they were to keep their distance, socially, from their students. However, the second semester he had only grading duties, and she wasn't in that class.

Joe ate, always alone, in one of the dining halls. The meals were filling but not to the point that they encouraged obesity. One day late in the second semester, he was having dinner when someone sat down opposite him. Joe looked up. It was Stacey.

"Hi, Joe," she said.

Joe sat, paralyzed. *Should I call her Stacey, Miss Porter, what?* He finally replied with "Hello."

She smiled in a friendly, reassuring way and began eating. After another awkward minute, Joe did the same.

"Are you TA'ing again?" asked Stacey.

Joe managed to swallow whatever it was, drank something, and said, "No. Well, yes. That is, I'm grading for the Intro Biology For Nonmajors class."

Joe was going to make some clever remark but couldn't think of anything to say, so he said nothing.

Stacey didn't seem put off and said, "I'm a premed. I've been admitted here. This place is the cheapest. I still haven't paid off my undergraduate loans. Have you?"

Joe forced himself to concentrate on the conversation. He was surprised at her asking such a personal question, but he didn't really mind. "I had a scholarship," he said. "That paid tuition. My folks helped out with room and board, and I worked during the summers. In fact, I don't owe anything for undergraduate school."

"What about grad school?"

"I have a federal fellowship. It pays for four years of tuition and expenses. If I have to stay longer than that to get my PhD, either whoever I work for has to have a grant or I have to pay my own way. But that is two years away. I work in the summer for an outfit called GeneQuestion. The pay there is pretty good, so I'm not worried."

"Once you get your PhD, what then? Can you get a job right away?"

Joe drank some milk and replied, "No, not an academic job. For that, I have to do postdoctoral work for I don't know how long and I don't know how many places. Then I would start as assistant professor and try desperately to get a research grant so I can publish enough to make tenure. And it is getting harder to get grants."

Joe thought about what he had said and then smiled at Stacey. "But it's my dream—a foolish dream, I guess—and I just have to give it my best shot. At least *you* are guaranteed a job when you get out."

Stacey nodded, got up, and smiled at Joe. Joe smiled back anxiously, wondering if he had said something she didn't like and if he had, what it was. But she gave Joe a friendly wave and walked away, her perfectly shaped hips swaying. That was very entertaining. He could just see the outline of her panties. The male undergraduates of the genetics lab Joe had supervised spent a lot of time speculating about whether Stacy wore them. Joe stared as long as she was in sight and then finished his meal. He had classes and labs of his own to attend.

Despite Joe's fears, Stacey again joined him for lunch the next day. This time, she asked, "Did I bore you with my problems? If I did, I apologize."

Joe shook his head; in fact, Stacey could have talked about a planned purchase of shoes or a handbag and he would have been enthralled.

Joe said, "It's a major worry of yours, so go ahead and talk about it. I'm here to listen."

Stacey smiled at Joe and began eating.

After a few minutes, she asked Joe, "Are your folks from Reno? Do they live here?"

Joe shook his head and replied, "My mom and dad live in Detroit—well, near the city. Dad worked for Ford, but he'll be retiring soon."

"Making cars?" asked Stacey.

"Bookkeeper for a Ford dealership," Joe answered. "Do your folks live in Nevada?"

Stacey shook her head. "Divorced. Some time back. I don't have much contact with either of them, haven't for several years."

Joe nodded sympathetically. "How about summer work?"

Stacey said, "I sell stationery. I make enough to live just through the summer, but that's about it. Have you ever thought about working full time for GeneQuestion? Would you make that much more as a professor?"

Joe shook his head. He remarked, "You don't go into the professor business to make money. I mean, the pay isn't bad, I understand you make a comfortable living, but people who go into the academic life have to really want to do that and nothing else."

There was silence while Joe ate several spoonfuls of soup out of a can, a big can, before he resumed. "If I was to leave school this semester, I would have to give up the federal fellowship, disappoint my boss, and get a MS. With that, well ...."

There was silence while Joe thought about what he was going to say.

"I could get a job as deputy director, meaning I would do all the work."

There was more silence, and then Joe finished, "In fact, I've heard a slot as deputy director will be open this summer. Here, I mean, in the Carson City branch."

Both Joe and Stacey ate some toast.

"How much does that pay?"

"Depending on experience, maybe eighty a year."

After a few moments, Joe added, "But I understand it is a tough job—I mean, emotionally wearing and takes a lot of time, ten–twelve hours a day, maybe fifty hours or more a week. Some days there is more work."

"Is it a good company to work for?"

Joe nodded. "Yeah, in many ways."

"What kind of life are you looking for, Joe?"

Joe looked sadly at Stacey and told her, "Nothing fancy, I guess: a place of my own, wife, kids, a place to come home to, a home, a refuge, a family, a nest."

Joe looked at his tray. "Decent meals—that's what I want."

They both laughed, and Joe asked, "You?"

Stacey looked off in the distance before replying. "The same, I guess. But mostly I don't want to have to worry about money. I want to be comfortable. I don't want to work behind a counter; I've had enough of that."

There was silence, and then Stacey resumed talking. "Having to stand there while people look and look and talk and talk, trying to be pleasant while they make up their minds, waiting and waiting, and maybe they buy something or maybe not. God, it's so frustrating, being so totally dependent on others! As a doctor, they will come to me, and I'll decide what they need, what they should do."

"But that's a lot of responsibility," Joe objected.

"I suppose."

They finished their meals in silence. Joe was struggling with the urge to ask Stacey out, maybe to a movie, maybe just dinner, when Stacey got up, gave Joe a brief nod, and walked away. Once more, Joe wondered if he had said something she didn't like. Was it that bit about being responsible for the patient's treatment? But she must understand that. Anyway, classes called.

That evening, coming back from the library, Joe saw a couple approaching: a tall man, with his arm about the shoulders of the woman with him. She had her arm around his waist. They were walking very close to each other. Then Joe recognized the woman: it was Stacey. As they came closer, Joe nodded to her. She seemed a little taken aback at seeing Joe.

Once past them, Joe heard the man say, "Who was that little creep?"

Stacey laughed and said, "A TA from a class last semester."

Joe reached his dorm room. He was heartsick. He put his books down and went to the men's room. He stared into the mirror. He wasn't really "little," just about average height, light build, with otherwise nondescript brownish hair and watery blue eyes. Nothing special. Joe sighed. Some things he just couldn't change.

He knew he should read, but instead he undressed, crawled into bed, and tried to sleep. He just wanted to escape, but all he could think about was class work. It was all he had in his life, probably all he ever would have. After a while, Joe finally fell asleep.

Joe had to give his own seminar in three weeks. That meant he had to do a lot of reading, a lot of writing, and, since his topic was on "DNA sequences associated with specific human characteristics, appearance, metabolism, and diseases," he had to go to the GeneQuestion office to get the most up-to-date, practical information. While there, he talked to the deputy director, who was in fact cleaning out his office. Joe introduced himself.

The man said, "Oh yeah, my replacement. When can you start?"

Joe said, "I haven't decided yet to leave the PhD program. Why are you leaving?"

The man tossed some things in a trash can and answered

Joe's question. "The job pays well, and the company is a decent one to work for, but I just got burned out. So I'm going back to school, get a doctorate, and maybe teach at a private school. That's what my wife wants me to do, and I finally decided she was right."

Joe nodded and left with the man's contact information. Over the next two weeks, he worked very hard. He kept eating at the dining hall, but didn't see Stacey. He didn't really expect to, but eating alone seemed lonelier than before.

Finally he was ready to write up his talk. It consisted of a description of his seminar, including references, figures, and tables, for people to keep and read if they wanted to. Then Joe prepared his PowerPoint slides. He had been told to keep them to fifteen or fewer for an hour-long talk. By the day of the seminar, he was ready and had printed copies for everyone.

He was finishing his lunch when Stacey appeared and sat down.

"Hi, Joe."

Joe looked steadily at her, then finished his milk, wiped his mouth and got up. "My seminar's today and I have to prepare," he told her.

And he left. He didn't bother to look back. He really did have to get set up and had just managed it when people began coming in.

His seminar was a big success. He had everything well organized and clear. He was even able to point out where the field was going. At the end of the hour, Joe found that the demand for the paper copies exceeded the supply, so he had to run off more. After that he had an afternoon class, and then the day was over.

Joe's faculty adviser/major professor/dissertation adviser was Herschel Markowitz, known to everyone as "Hersh." He was about Joe's size, dark haired, and came from New York City. He still spoke with a New York accent. In spite of this, he seemed very much at home in Nevada. Hersh invited Joe to have dinner with him.

The professor explained, "My wife is having a hen party, so I was invited to stay away until it was over."

"Any chance of reasonable leftovers?" asked Joe.

"Not the way those women eat," Hersh said. "Pizza okay?"

Joe nodded. Hersh drove the two of them to a Papa John's, where they ordered and then sat down in a booth.

While they waited for their food, Hersh said, "That was a damn good talk, Joe. Well researched, well delivered, very professional."

Joe was drinking a Coke. Hersh's praise was comforting, but Joe had to tell him what was on his mind, about dropping out with an MS and getting a job, so he started talking about his new career plan. "I've got an offer as deputy director of the GeneQuestion lab in Carson City," he told Hersh. "The pay is good, and the company lets its people go to school on their own time."

Their pizzas arrived. They ate in silence a few minutes.

"I can't say I blame you," Hersh said. "If I was in your position today, I would be damn reluctant to take the academic track. The bean counters and suits in administration consider only one thing: grant dollars. Easy to measure. And the indirect costs keep those people afloat, no matter what they tell Congress. Still, if it's your dream, you have to follow it."

"Would I be able to finish my PhD here, taking one course a semester, at my own expense, of course? With a PhD, I could get a job as director, here or someplace else."

"What dissertation topic?"

Joe shook his head and said, "I would need your advice on that. Maybe something I could use the GeneQuestion equipment for—with their permission, I mean."

Joe's adviser nodded but said, "Give this some serious thought, Joe. I really think it's better to get the degree you signed up for, and then look around. The grant situation may ease, but I can't say I see that happening."

Joe nodded. The men finished their pizzas. Then Hersh drove Joe back to his dorm room.

The next day, Joe was eating lunch when Stacey sat down opposite him with her tray. "How did the talk go, Joe?" she asked.

Joe looked at her a little warily but was still feeling happy about the praise he had gotten, so he replied. "Everyone thought it was very good. I passed the hat for donations, but I didn't get any. Then someone stole the hat."

Joe drank some milk while Stacey stared at him. Then she realized Joe had made a joke, and smiled. It was amazing, how that smile lit up her face. Joe had to smile in return, while reminding himself about the "little creep" remark that Stacey hadn't objected to. And if she had a boyfriend, why was she talking to Joe?

"Are you going to celebrate?" Stacey asked.

Joe shook his head. "My boss took me out for pizza. I reckon that's all the celebrating I'll be doing."

"There's a rerun of *The Maltese Falcon* showing tonight at the student union," Stacey said. "You want to go? I'll spring for the tickets."

This time it was Joe's turn to stare. Was she actually asking him, Joe Stallings, out on a date? He decided to play along.

"Sure," he said. "When do you want me to come by?"

He was thinking she was going to say, "Not in this lifetime."

But instead she told Joe, "Come by my dorm at seven. The show starts at seven thirty."

Joe could only say, "Okay."

Late that afternoon Joe got cleaned up, shaved again, put on deodorant, and climbed into his best clothes. He appeared at the dorm promptly on time and was surprised to see Stacey waiting in the lobby.

"Am I late?" asked Joe, checking his watch.

"No," replied Stacey. "I just came down."

Looking at Stacey, Joe was swept away. She was dazzling.

"Damn," said Joe. "I should have brought my sword to keep all the other guys from carrying you off."

Stacey looked surprised for a few seconds before she smiled

sweetly at Joe in response to his compliment. Joe felt his knees go weak, but he managed to open the dorm door for her. They walked together to the student union.

As promised, Stacey paid for the tickets and they went inside. In spite of the legendary status of *The Maltese Falcon*, the place was only about a third full. They sat down together. Stacey's perfume was nothing short of bewitching. Joe became aroused. His embarrassment about when he would have to stand up distracted him from the movie. When the movie ended, Joe didn't know what to do. He got up quickly and half turned from Stacey, leading her toward the exit and hoping no one noticed. Finally they were out in the cooling night air. Joe could almost swear Stacey was staring at his crotch, but things were subsiding now.

Joe looked toward her and asked, "Something to eat? I can probably manage that."

Stacey replied, "I didn't eat at the dining hall. I really couldn't take ham loaf again. I think the Burger King is open."

"Me either, and for the same reason, but I think they're going to keep serving ham loaf until they use it up. Then they'll make some more."

Stacey laughed, and Joe was encouraged to offer her his arm. After some hesitation, Stacey took Joe's arm and Joe walked proudly with her to the Burger King.

While they were eating, Stacey asked Joe whether he had made a decision yet.

"I'm still wavering," Joe confessed. "My faculty adviser was sympathetic. I don't think he feels there is much future in academic life either. He just told me to give the matter a lot of thought. The deputy director at the GeneQuestion lab said in effect that he was burned out."

"How long had he been doing it?"

"Ten, fifteen years, I think."

They finished their meals, and then Joe escorted Stacey back to campus, intending to take her to her dorm. Stacey took Joe's arm, pulling him close. Joe was becoming aroused again.

Stacey asked Joe, "Where do you stay?"

"In the graduate dorm."

"Is that a nicer place?"

Joe shrugged and said, "The only difference is that it's filled with grad students, so it's quieter."

"I'd like to see your room, Joe."

Joe didn't know what to think about this, but forced himself to take her words at face value.

"If you are interested in squalor, I can satisfy your taste. Otherwise, well, you can judge for yourself."

Joe supposed she was thinking of living there instead of one of the women's dorms.

They walked to the graduate dorm and went to Joe's room. Joe unlocked the door, turned on the light, and, with a gesture, invited Stacey inside.

Despite Joe's remarks, looking around his room he could see that it was reasonably clean. The trash can was emptied, and the bed was made—sort of. The only clutter was from stacks of books and papers on the desk. Stacey didn't comment on the room, just began unbuttoning her blouse. She kept her eyes on Joe's crotch as she did so, and wasn't disappointed. Joe was completely aroused as he stared at Stacey's bra. Stacey began unhooking it, and left it with her blouse on Joe's desk.

For a moment, the words of a song from *Oklahoma* ran through Joe's mind: "Everything she had was absolutely real." No padded bra. Joe extended his hands to Stacey's breasts and began fondling them. They were soft but firm, full but did not sag. The nipples were light colored and large. Then Stacey unzipped her skirt and stepped out of it and her shoes. She pulled her panties down and stepped out of those as well.

Joe began to undress too. The whole business seemed only partly real; he wondered if he was dreaming. Stacey lay down on Joe's bed and spread her legs. Joe was having trouble undressing: pieces of his clothing weren't cooperating, partly because he was aroused. He became impatient, tearing some things in the process. Finally he was naked, or naked enough. Joe climbed onto the bed and approached Stacey. Despite the advice he remembered hearing from men claiming to be more experienced—"Think about baseball"—Joe discharged as soon as he entered her.

Joe remained lying on Stacey a few minutes, hoping something else would happen, but nothing did, so he rolled off and lay sweating next to her. He felt totally embarrassed, completely humiliated. He tried to think of something to say.

Finally, absurdly, he said, "Will you marry me?"

And Stacey replied, "Sure, Joe."

That was all, but Joe slowly realized that he and Stacey were going to marry. As he lay there, the implications became obvious to him.

"I'll have to take that GeneQuestion job then. I'd better check, to be sure they're going to hire me. Then I'll have to tell my major professor, fill out the paperwork to get the master's degree, and get him to sign it."

"When do you want to get married?" Stacey asked.

Joe thought and replied, "As soon as possible, I guess. We'll have to move, once the semester is over. Unless you want to live in married-student housing."

"No."

"We'll need cars, each of us. And I'll get you a ring."

Stacey turned to Joe and Joe turned to her, and they kissed. So it was all decided.

MARRIED BLISS

The next day was Saturday, and Joe and Stacey married in the office of a justice of the peace. On their way there, they stopped at a jewelry store, and Joe paid nearly $1,000 for a ring. Stacey beamed her approval at him as she flashed it on her hand. After they were married, they moved Stacey's things into Joe's dorm room, since there was plenty of space. At least, there was until Stacey moved in. For someone in considerable debt, Joe thought she had a very big wardrobe, though not much jewelry.

Stacey allowed Joe to make love to her again. As she was getting dressed, Joe watched her. "You are perfection," he said. "You are Venus. You are my Venus."

Stacey smiled briefly at Joe, and they went out to have dinner at a nearby Chinese restaurant. Until they got cars, they were limited to places close to the dorm. At the restaurant, Stacey gave Joe a list of her student loans and told him how much tuition at the medical school would cost.

On Monday Joe applied for the position of deputy director at the GeneQuestion lab and was assured the job was his, provided he had a master's degree. Joe then told his professor what he had decided to do. Hersh frowned, but signed the paperwork allowing Joe to take a terminal master's. As Joe left, he could see his professor slowly and sadly shaking his head. For a moment Joe wanted to go back to being his grad student, but he had given Stacey his word. She was his wife, and he thought he had to do everything he could to support her dreams. So he took the signed forms to administration.

Joe also wrote to the National Science Foundation, giving up his federal fellowship. Then he and Stacey shopped for two multihand cars and looked for an apartment, since there were no cheap places near GeneQuestion. Stacey asked for a new car, but Joe told her that right now, an extensively used but functional Ford Escort was all they could afford. Stacey scowled. They found a reasonable apartment that would be available after finals. Unfortunately, a security deposit was required, which Joe paid. After finals, Joe and Stacey settled into their new life together. Joe got Stacey a job answering the phone and setting up appointments at GeneQuestion. For the summer, at least, they would be working together.

The lab director handled giving the bad news to customers. Joe watched. Otherwise, Joe was in charge of the equipment, orders, and maintenance. He consulted the director often. Stacey's job performance was okay, so Joe and Stacey became a two-income couple. But there was a problem: Stacey insisted on keeping her old bank account privately online, and didn't add his name to the account. Joe found this disquieting: he knew this was the custom in some families, but he didn't like keeping things like that secret, not when he was paying off her loans. But he said nothing because he loved her.

Monday through Saturday, Joe and Stacey were together all day. Sometimes they made sandwiches and had lunch together; sometimes Stacey would use her car to get something during her lunch break. On Sundays they had breakfast at an IHOP and then went to a coin laundry with their dirty clothes. While the washer or dryer was going, Joe read technical manuals using his laptop. Stacey would send or receive e-mails with her iPad or do her nails. Then they got lunch, often Chinese. The usual surplus was put in the refrigerator for the evening meal. Then, with nothing much else to do, they would make love.

By exercising maximum self-control, Joe was able to satisfy Stacey sexually. Or so it appeared. Stacey confirmed this by complimenting Joe on his performance. Because Joe was aware that Stacey was sexually experienced, this pleased him a lot, though he would wonder, from time to time, how many sex partners she had had. Also, why had she picked Joe? Because he had asked her to marry him and the other men hadn't? Or was there another reason? Joe tried to focus on the life he was living with Stacey and just make the most of it. He had never had a girlfriend, or for that matter a date before Stacey, and now he had a wife. He just had to learn the ropes.

Joe was taking home about $5,000 a month. For medical school tuition that fall, never mind expenses, Stacey would need about sixteen thousand. Joe talked to her about it, and she suggested Joe use his credit card or take out a student loan. Joe knew Stacey was taking home about a thousand a month from GeneQuestion. He was a little nettled: wasn't Stacey prepared to contribute anything? Joe and Stacey's living expenses— rent, food, and utilities—came to about a thousand a month. There would be a $4,000 shortfall. Also, Stacey insisted on an allowance of $150 a week. She wasn't too clear about what it was for, although Joe assumed it was for books and food at the medical school. Stacey did promise to cut her spending on clothes and cosmetics. Joe shook his head. He told Stacey things were going to be tight for the first year or so and that she should just try to avoid going further into debt. Once Joe paid off some of the interest on Stacey's loans, their taxes should be lower, so a few thousand could be recovered. Stacey looked unconcerned as she listened to him. Joe would find a way.

In the end, Joe had to use his credit card. He calculated he could pay off the medical school tuition debt before having to pay interest. And that is what he did. Once Stacey was in medical school, Joe began living on marked-down canned soups and stew washed down with house-brand discount soft drinks bought by the case and supplemented with loss-leader candy bars purchased in bulk. This certainly cut Joe's expenses. It also ensured that although he might gain some weight, he wasn't going to enjoy doing it.

Week followed week. Joe was slowly being given a more and more important role in all aspects of the business, not just the technical ones. The director was also planning to retire, and wanted Joe to fill in until a new director was hired. So Joe sat in when the director gave the clients the results. Lonely and withdrawn as Joe was, he didn't like seeing clients' emotional reactions to the news they had to hear. He tried very hard to be detached, but it was a struggle. Joe was much better and much happier with the technical part of the job: it was mechanical, predictable, scientific, and remote from the pain and heartache of human beings. Except, of course, when things weren't working. But the equipment could be fixed, unlike the problems of the clients.

By the end of Stacey's first year of med school, Joe had managed to pay all of her expenses and had several thousand dollars left over. The couple spent the summer as before. Once more, Stacey put her salary in her account while Joe earned her second-year tuition. Joe tried not to resent Stacey's attitude. He tried not to question or judge. Stacey was his wife, and he had to support her aims to the best of his ability.

During the first semester of her second year, Joe read Stacey's human genetics textbook on Sundays in the Laundromat. This was to bone up on the genetic diseases some of the clients' children had, the treatments (always awkward), and prognoses (almost always bad). Stacey didn't object. After all, Joe was paying for her books, and paying a lot. The cost of those things startled Joe. Even so, he managed to get a little further ahead on Stacey's tuition.

Stacey's third year would consist of clinical rounds, so her schedule would be shifting and uncertain. However, she had to pass Part One of the Medical Boards at the end of her second year. Joe could tell she was worried and did what he could to support her. When she learned she had passed, with a respectable score so she could continue, she wanted to celebrate.

Since it was near their second anniversary, Joe bought Stacey a silver pin in the shape of a flower. He wasn't sure what the flower was, so he asked the woman behind the counter.

"A cactus flower," she told Joe.

Joe thought a moment and then decided to buy it. It was very pretty (and expensive), and Stacey was a rather prickly character. He wasn't sure he could tell her that, so he just paid and continued shopping.

Joe also bought a bottle of good sparkling wine. Stacey liked wine. The label on the bottle said Brut. Joe wasn't sure what that meant, but he and Stacey had drunk wine from this same vineyard before, so he bought it. And he bought a couple of good steaks from a "to-go" place, cooked the way Stacey liked them, along with mashed potatoes and gravy. He headed back to their apartment, figuring to make Stacey even happier. It was not too late, even though Saturdays were the busiest days at GeneQuestion; Joe had managed to get off a little early.

Stacey had apparently started celebrating already, judging by the smell of alcohol and the fact she was slumped over the table. She roused herself when Joe came in with his bags. The smell of the food filled their little kitchen.

"T-bones, potatoes, and gravy," explained Joe. "May need reheating. And ...."

Here Joe presented the bottle of wine. Stacey inspected the label, but clearly was not very impressed.

What in hell had she been drinking? Joe wondered.

After fumbling around, Stacey started the microwave to reheat the steaks. Joe set the table. He also set the little box with the pin next to Stacey's plate. He poured glasses of wine for them both. Stacey sat heavily down on the chair Joe held for her, and then began drinking the wine. She finished the glass. Joe poured another and rescued the T-bones, which were popping. He put the potatoes and gravy in the microwave and started it.

Joe sat down opposite Stacey, who, between mouthfuls of tenderloin, had seen the box. She lifted her eyes to Joe, who raised his glass of wine to her, smiling. After a minute, Stacey smiled back and raised her glass, now nearly empty, to him.

"Congratulations, and happy second wedding anniversary," Joe said.

Stacey looked confused. After Joe filled her glass once more, the microwave went off. Joe got the potatoes and gravy, set them on hot pads on the table, and served some of each to Stacey. He took some himself. The gravy was thin but very flavorful. Stacey opened the box and stared at the pin. She took it out and looked it over carefully, and then looked at him.

"Thanks, Joe."

He affected a Humphrey Bogart rasp: "Stick with me, kid, and you'll go around bedecked like some pagan goddess."

She smiled and drank some more wine. They finished the steaks, more than half the potatoes and gravy, and nearly two-thirds of the bottle of wine. Joe carefully put the rest of the potatoes and gravy away and made some sketchy attempts at clearing the table. Stacey had gone to the bathroom. Joe felt tired. He hadn't drunk nearly as much as Stacey, but it had still made him sleepy. He changed into a bathrobe and headed for the bed. Then Joe heard the toilet flush, and Stacey came into the bedroom. She was naked.

Joe's sleepiness disappeared. He caressed Stacey's breasts. He saw something new: her nipples were erect. Also, she began breathing heavily. So Joe mounted his wife and began intercourse. In the past, Stacey had signaled her orgasms, or what Joe had assumed were her orgasms, by moaning and turning her head back and forth. Tonight was different: she was not so much breathing as gasping. She was grunting, making guttural sounds to Joe's thrusts. Then she began shaking all over before Joe had finished.

Joe realized they were both sweating, not just him. He got off Stacey and lay down next to her, wondering what was happening. He turned toward her and tried to kiss her, but Stacey pushed him away, hard. She almost hit him. Joe lay there, feeling his shoulder hurting, too appalled to speak. This was simply not tolerable behavior. Joe's silence seemed to register with Stacey, but instead of apologizing or attempting to explain, she got up and went into the kitchen, then the bathroom. She not only closed the door but locked it.

Joe didn't know what to do. Eventually, he got up and went into the kitchen. In the kitchen, he could smell the wine. He looked in the sink and realized Stacey had poured some down the drain. The empty bottle was in the trash. Joe did not understand: he thought Stacey had liked the wine. Certainly she had drunk at least half the bottle. But Joe didn't think he could ask Stacey about it.

Joe washed the dishes from their meal. Then he sat down where they had eaten and drank a glass of milk, trying to sort out what had happened. Had he hurt Stacey? That didn't seem likely, but without her telling Joe what was wrong, he was at sea. He heard the bathroom door open. Stacey came out but didn't stop to speak to Joe; she just went to bed. After a few minutes, Joe joined her. Stacey had rolled herself in a cocoon of blankets, leaving nothing for Joe. Joe scowled, fished a fresh blanket out of the dresser, folded it in half, and covered himself with it. He slept.

The next morning, Sunday, Joe and Stacey got dressed. Stacey put the silver flower pin on, and they went to IHOP. Stacey's mood seemed improved when three women—a waitress and two customers—commented on the pin. "It's an anniversary present from my husband," she said happily, nodding at Joe.

"Your husband has good taste," said one of the customers.

In the Laundromat, two other women noticed the pin, and

there were remarks to the effect that if Joe could come up with something that nice for the second anniversary, Stacey would be overwhelmed by what Joe got for their tenth or, even better, their twenty-fifth.

Joe smiled and said, "I guess I'll need to start saving now," at which the admirers laughed, as well as Stacey.

After the clothes were dried and folded, Joe suggested lunch at Golden Corral. Stacey was clearly happy with this idea, so they went there. Once more, several women were impressed by Stacey's pin, one of them remarking that Stacey was "a lucky woman," clearly referring to Joe. Stacey basked in the admiration, even smiling at Joe two or three times, so it was a very pleasant lunch. The food wasn't bad either.

Joe kept thinking he should insist on an explanation, but slowly he realized that he wasn't going to get one—at least an honest one. So the day passed, and the days following, and their lives returned to routine. Still, the memory of that night stayed with Joe; it was a burr under the matrimonial saddle. If that was all, well, Joe could accept what had happened even if he didn't understand it. Or maybe he was reluctant to try to figure it out.

But there was something else that Joe had noticed. Stacey had two friends, female medical students. They treated Joe with an amused contempt. This irritated him, but it also made him wonder if their attitudes weren't a reflection of Stacey's.

The three women sometimes gathered in Joe and Stacey's apartment for drinks and talk before Joe got home from work. Joe shopped around for a voice-activated recorder. He was aware that women often shared secrets that men would almost never talk about. He was also aware that Stacey would be outraged if she discovered what he was doing. Consequently, Joe used duct tape to attach the recorder to the underside of a table in the apartment. He had to take time off from work, a time when Stacey was doing her clinical rounds, but he was prepared to make up the time.

Joe began having lunch at the apartment to hear the women's

conversations. Several days went by without a gathering, and then he hit pay dirt—in more than one sense.

One of Stacey's friends said, "This is good wine. It tastes expensive."

"It is," Stacey said. "So I don't show it to Macho Man."

The other two women laughed. Then Joe realized that Macho Man was Stacey's private name for him.

"He's so insecure," remarked the other friend.

"With good reason," returned Stacey, and they all laughed once more.

"How much longer are you going to have to put up with him?" the first woman asked.

"He's paid almost half my debts," Stacey said. "There is an installment due just now. After he's paid them all, I'll kiss him good-bye in, say, two years."

"Then it's off to LA with Trevor?" the other woman asked.

"Yes," Stacey said. "Nooners at the Comstock Motel are wonderful, but they're no substitute for marriage. Trev has his eye on a set of suites in a medical office complex where we can set up a practice together. He'll have to divorce that nurse-wife of his first, of course."

There was silence while the three women drank the wine. Joe sat, stunned. His worst fears were realized, or perhaps confirmed.

Then the first woman remarked, "Trevor's wife was telling me she wants to have a baby once Trevor finishes his residency."

"He's a baby-maker, no doubt about it," Stacey said. The three women laughed again, and then Stacey added, "With Trevor I sure don't have to fake my orgasms."

"Wow," one of them women said and then suggested, "Let's have lunch at El Ranchero."

There were sounds of agreement, and then the first woman asked Stacey, "Doesn't your insignificant other ever question your expenses?"

"He doesn't dare," returned Stacey. There was more laughter, and then silence.

For a few minutes, Joe knew what it felt like to want to murder someone. If he had a gun ... but he didn't. And he didn't want to go to prison ... He had to get back to work. But first he looked for Stacey's hiding place for the wine. He soon located it, and he could guess that it was indeed expensive. For that matter, El Ranchero was the most expensive place in town. That miserable, greedy, faithless bitch! But what could Joe do?

Joe got into his beat-up second- or third-hand Ford Ranger pickup and started the engine. Then he came to a decision, turned off the engine, and went back into their apartment. He took the recorder off the bottom of the table, crumpling up the duct tape he had used to attach it. Outside, he threw the ball of duct tape into a Dumpster, got back into the truck, put the recorder on the seat next to him, started the engine, and headed back to where he worked.

The more he thought about his life with Stacey, the more obvious everything was. Stacey had seduced Joe and married him for his money. Obvious? Sure, except Joe had fallen completely, totally, in love with her.

As he drove, it occurred to Joe that Trevor, whoever he was, was cut from the same cloth as Stacey: selfish and exploitative. He briefly wondered if Trevor was stringing Stacey along just as Stacey was stringing Joe along. Well, that was her problem. Joe needed to get Trevor's last name and then hire a divorce attorney—the best available. The latest installment to pay Stacey's medical school debts would go to pay for a divorce instead. Joe smiled at that thought as he pulled into the parking lot where he worked. As he parked, he considered he might have to hire a private detective too but he decided to let the lawyer deal with that.

There was some business to be done, which Joe attended to, all routine, though critically important to the clients. Joe spoke to each of them, wondering if the results of the paternity tests might trigger a murder. Joe was feeling much more sympathetic toward his clients. As soon as the tests were set up for those who had brought samples of the children's saliva (the tests also checked for inherited diseases—that was the excuse men offered their wives), Joe looked up the staff at the hospital attached to the medical school where Stacey was still a student. He soon found a doctor doing his residency named Trevor, Trevor Eastman. Joe wrote down the name and then looked at the listings for divorce lawyers.

Joe knew a few divorced people, some from the lab where he worked. He canvassed them, asking for recommendations. Joe pretended he was doing it for a friend, but guessed no one was fooled. One name was given as the best and most expensive. Joe said he would pass the information along to his friend and that he thought the divorce would be pretty routine. More knowing nods. Realizing he needed something to eat, he pulled a can of stew out of his desk along with a spoon, a bowl, and an opener. It wasn't El Ranchero, not by a long way, but it was growing late in the day.

After microwaving the stew and eating it, washing it down with water from the water fountain in the hall, Joe called the attorney's office. The man himself answered, and Joe told him his problem. The lawyer told Joe his fee just for a consultation, a sum that made Joe wince, but to which he agreed. The lawyer told Joe to come over.

The attorney's office was very impressive: heavy, rich-colored furniture, and nearly every wall lined with bookshelves filled with law books. Joe played the recording of the women's conversation. The lawyer took one or two notes. Joe told the man who he thought Trevor was. The lawyer made another note and then asked Joe for payment. Joe had to use his credit card, but he was well below the credit limit, and paid.

Then the lawyer, now Joe's lawyer, told him, "Give me your wife's license plate number and a description of her car, and I'll have a detective follow her to the Comstock Motel, to document her activities."

Joe gave the information and then left, feeling he was taking action though still mourning the loss of a dream. Fortunately, Stacey was on night duty—or so she had told Joe.

Over the next two days, Joe worked very hard to avoid talking to Stacey, using work as his excuse. Stacey twice reminded Joe of the debt payment, and Joe nodded reassuringly.

Then, on a Friday afternoon, Joe got a call from the lawyer, who said, "We got them both. I have the divorce papers ready for serving. When do you want to break the bad news?"

Joe said, "Now. I'll move out this afternoon. You have my work number and address."

"Right," said the lawyer, ending the conversation, and it was done. Joe's marriage had lasted less than two and a half years.

A Research Project

Joe returned to the University of Nevada with the bone sample. From Winnemucca to Reno is about 160 miles, less than two hours at normal (Nevada) driving speeds. Joe was in a hurry to start. He was using his two weeks of vacation, so he took things a little fast. He was driving his new pickup, a big, powerful Ford F-150, which had air-conditioning.

"Screw the environment," said Joe as he turned it on.

Just west of Winnemucca, I-80 turned roughly southwest. Past Lovelock, the road lay in a valley between the Trinity Range to the northwest and the Humboldt Range to the southeast. The Humboldt River ran to the north of the interstate, but now turned under the highway. Never very large, the Humboldt would disappear into the ground in the Humboldt Sink, just a few miles southwest of Lovelock. This was the last of the world that those forty or fifty human beings saw before being chased into the cave where they had suffocated—how long ago?

There was also a railroad that followed I-80 most of the way to Reno. An Amtrak train was on it, but unfortunately it was heading east, so Joe couldn't race it.

Near Reno, Joe turned into a Burger King, got a number one

combo, and drove to the building housing the Department of Genetics. He parked and took the tooth and his meal into the building. Hersh was there, though preparing to leave.

"Got it?" he asked.

Joe held up the bag with the meal. Both men grinned, and then Joe showed his professor the tooth in its container. Hersh seemed impressed by its size. He nodded, and told Joe, "Good luck."

Hersh had also suggested the topic for Joe's last seminar: "Sequencing of Ancient DNA (aDNA)." Joe had gotten both a theoretical knowledge and a very good practical knowledge of the field, including how to run the "next generation" DNA sequencer. Hersh had been one of the authors of a grant proposal to the National Science Foundation for money to acquire the sequencer.

Miraculously, they had gotten the money and bought the instrument, which was kept in Hersh's lab because there was room for it there. Joe had read the manual and was confident he could run it. Joe had paid for supplies such as the streptavidin-coated beads and the biotinylated adapter DNA "primers" because Hersh didn't have any more grant money. Joe had also bought the flow cell upon which the DNA fragments would be spread out. This model was considered the best. It was also the most expensive. With all the enzymes and other things needed, Joe wound up sinking most of two months of take-home pay into the project. If the project was a success, he wouldn't regret a dime of it. But Joe had just two weeks to sink or swim.

Joe first turned on the sterile room's filtered air supply. Then he ate the burger. After that, he went to the departmental liquid nitrogen tank with Hersh's metal thermos and a pair of asbestos gloves. He filled the thermos and carried it and its bubbling contents back to the lab. There he set the thermos and the jar with the tooth on the revolving access port, put on a Tyvek suit, and went into the sterile room.

Joe washed the tooth three times in a mild detergent solution made with water that had been deionized, then distilled, then filtered through a Millipore filter that removed all bacteria. The tooth was then rinsed three times in just the water. Joe gripped the tooth with sterile tweezers, set it in a sterile stainless steel dish, and poured liquid nitrogen over it.

Joe prepared the mill for grinding up the tooth and set out the special small-volume centrifuge tubes. They had inserts containing porous silica plates set in the bottoms of the inserts. Now Joe began to grind up the tooth in the mill.

After reducing the tooth to a fine slurry in the EDTA-proteinase K-containing extraction solution, Joe left the slurry to sit overnight at thirty-seven degrees. At this point, he cleaned up everything he wouldn't need the next day and then went to the small conference room where there was a table, some chairs, and a sofa with a pillow and a blanket. Joe set his alarm clock, took off his shoes, emptied his pockets, turned out the lights, made his way to the sofa, and fell asleep.

The next day, Joe centrifuged the digested, extracted bone slurry. He poured off the liquid, added a binding buffer containing guanidine hydrochloride to the liquid and centrifuged this through the silica plates in the inserts of the centrifuge tubes. This was basically to separate contaminating human and bacterial DNA (large) from the presumably fragmented DNA (small) from the tooth.

Joe rinsed whatever was bound to the silica three times with the binding buffer and then put the inserts into fresh tubes. He centrifuged two rinses of ethanol through the silica, and then replaced the centrifuge tubes once more. He now added water and centrifuged two small volumes of water through the silica. Now, he hoped, he had his DNA pieces.

All the DNA fragments, perhaps thousands of them, were spread out on the surface of the flow cell. Each DNA fragment was attached at one end to the beads on the surface of the flow cell through the streptavidin-biotin connection. Even with a large number of fragments, they were widely spaced on the surface.

They could all be copied many times using the polymerase chain reaction and still be seen as separate by the sequencer. The copying was to amplify the signal made in the actual DNA-sequencing reaction.

Then the original and polymerase chain reaction copied DNA strands were copied once more during the actual sequencing reactions. Each of the lengthening copies together produced a microdot of light under ultraviolet light. The light from each of the sequencing copies would have one of four colors. The color told the sequencer what DNA base was at the tip of the growing DNA-sequencing copy.

The computer controlling the sequencer identified the colors and measured the locations of all the microdots of light. It kept track of them; in fact, if only sequences from a particular organism were wanted, the instrument would discard the others once long-enough sequences were gotten. Joe of course wanted human.

Joe quit to get something to eat and then returned. Otherwise he worked around the clock over the next few days. There was no one else around: Joe was Hersh's only student because the professor couldn't afford to use anyone who didn't pay his or her own way.

Actually the idea behind the project came from Hersh, so he came into the lab often to check on its progress. One day, Hersh appeared with an offer to take Joe out to Steak 'n Shake for lunch.

Joe looked at his watch, shook his head in amazement, and commented, "Time sure flies when you're enjoying yourself."

His professor laughed, and clapped Joe on the shoulder.

They went out to eat, and when they came back, they had some sequences. Joe sat down to analyze the information, and the professor sat down with him. The sequences Joe had gotten from the DNA fragments were matched to the human genome, which would rule out contamination by bacteria or other nonhuman DNA. Joe and Hersh were delighted to find that there was indeed human DNA in Joe's preparation.

"A good start," said Hersh. Joe, greatly relieved, nodded.

Joe's turned his attention to the next hurdle: the DNA was human, but was the human the owner of the tooth or did the DNA belong to one or more of the unknown number of humans who had had some sort of contact with the skull? Joe knew there was only one way to find out. The DNA base cytosine spontaneously loses its amine group, becoming uracil. This registers as thymine in the sequence, a mistaken thymine, in the human reference DNA sequence. The rate of the spontaneous change is about 50 percent over five hundred years, a kind of chemical clock in fossil DNA. If the DNA fragments Joe was sequencing were ancient, he could get an idea of how ancient from the percent of spontaneous loss of the amine.

If the DNA was from someone who had lived during the past century, the extent of loss of the amine would be much less than 50 percent—around 10 or 20 percent.

Joe—and Hersh, when he had a free moment—looked carefully for "mistaken" thymine, relative to the known human DNA sequence. After three more days or so, they had their answer: the DNA sample had lost about 80 to 85 percent of the cytosines, meaning it was more than a thousand years old. Joe and Hersh high-fived and laughed, and each began his own dance around the lab. At this point, Joe could look for the characteristics of the owner of the tooth: eyes, hair color, and ethnicity.

After only a few hours, Joe could definitely say that the skull belonged to a male of European (or "Indo-European") ethnicity, and had blue eyes, red hair, and lactase persistence, which was also a characteristic of most modern Europeans. Provided a carbon 14 date could be obtained to back up the rough estimate from the cytosine loss, Joe had a story, and the basis for a dissertation and a published paper. All he needed to do now was repeat the sequencing.

He began right away: his two-week vacation was slipping away fast. Joe had been using his spare moments to write his dissertation, and it was well along. However, a carbon 14 date was absolutely necessary. Joe gave his professor the news and showed him the results, and the two men agreed to try to get another bone sample or perhaps dig around Lovelock Cave to see if Joe could find some other datable organic material. Hersh also handed him the heavily corrected, annotated first draft of the dissertation.

By the time Joe had to return to work, he was happier than he had been for a very long time. He had to revise his dissertation, but would do it at night and on Sundays. The pressure was off: he had nearly reached one of his major life goals.

Hersh seemed very happy, too. "Of all my students, you were the best," he said. "It killed me to send you off with a terminal master's degree. Damn, I'm happy for us both."

Joe was surprised and very moved. He sat down at his desk and decided to call Penny Echeverria, ostensibly to enlist her help. She had given him her card.

She was in. "Hello?"

"This is Joe Stallings. The skull is from a male European: blue eyes, red hair, and lactase persistence. What I need now is either another tooth for a carbon 14 date, or else your help with the Bureau of Land Management to dig around Lovelock Cave to try to get some organic fragment, hair, cloth, bone—anything with carbon in it. Are you willing to help?"

There was a moment of silence, and then Penny said, "Wow. You haven't wasted any time."

"I had just two weeks to do the work—my vacation, as a matter of fact—and now I'm going to finish writing my dissertation on what was found. In my abundant leisure time, of course. What I have is enough for the dissertation, but getting this other information would help you folks a lot."

It was quiet again, and then Penny said, "Give me your number and I'll talk to my boss."

Joe gave her his cell phone number and logged off. He was about to start the revisions to his dissertation when he remembered. He checked his phone for messages. Several were from work, routine things he would straighten out when he got back; otherwise there was nothing. That was still a relief, even after so many years.

His now ex-wife hadn't taken the divorce quietly. She was venomously angry, mixing insults with threats. Joe had recorded four examples among as many as thirty a day:

"Joe, you bastard, no one reneges on a promise to me. You miserable wimp, I have friends who can and will make your life a misery. I know where you work and what you drive."

"Joe, you cocksucker, you better watch your back. Sooner or later, my friends and I will catch up with you."

"Joe, whatever you have done to me, I'll see you paid back ten-fold, you miserable excuse for a man."

"Joe, you weren't much in bed, but when my friends catch you, you won't be a man at all."

Joe had gone to his lawyer, and the lawyer had gone to the judge who handled the divorce, and had gotten a restraining order. The order forbade Stacey from communicating with Joe in any fashion, and Joe had hoped that would settle things. It hadn't.

One evening, Joe got in his pickup to drive to his room. He started the engine and began to drive away when he heard two loud pops. Joe felt the truck shake and then settle. When he stopped and got out, he saw that two of his tires were flat. Joe had to call for a tow truck. At the garage he was towed to, he was shown two pieces of wood with a nail in one end. They had been placed where Joe wouldn't be likely to see them before driving away.

After that, Joe routinely used a stick to sweep for sharp things pointing toward his tires. He found some and managed to avoid more flats. Then someone threw a big rock at each truck window. Joe had to have all of them replaced, which was hard to do because Joe's truck was an older model. But a few days later, he found a side window broken out. The door was unlocked, and the truck wouldn't start. When Joe carefully opened the hood to see what had been done, he found the ignition wires all cut and the distributor cap gone. Finally Joe had had to sell the thing for scrap and buy the pickup he now drove.

Also, there were problems with the room Joe was renting. He was never able to figure out how Stacey had discovered where he was staying. Joe began to think he was being followed. One evening, late as usual, he came up to his room and saw that the door was open. Joe looked cautiously inside. Several glasses and dishes were lying on the floor, broken. Some books were lying on the floor. They had been kicked around, and the bindings were ruined. Joe got the landlord to change the lock, but someone forced the door, tore up some of Joe's shirts, and scattered his other clothes.

The last straw came when Joe's room was broken into and someone had defecated on the bed. Joe's clothes had been cut with scissors and crushed into the feces. His electric razor had been put in the toilet, and generally, everything Joe owned that was in that room had been ruined. The landlord had confiscated Joe's security deposit and told Joe to leave. Fortunately Joe had been smart enough to keep everything valuable or irreplaceable in his office at work, but he finally decided to move out of Carson City. He bought a lot, about ten acres, on one of the few patches of land not owned or controlled by the federal government. It was a few miles southeast of Carson City, in the hills, and lay next to a dry streambed named Gold Creek.

Joe bought an old camper—second-, third-, fourth-hand, no one could tell him how many owners it had had. But it was small enough and, Joe hoped, light enough that he could tow it to his lot. Joe was just able to move the thing there. Several times, he thought he was going to lose the engine of his pickup, but it was on his lot at last. Joe had kept a watch for anyone trying to follow him, though the dust track he left going the last few miles (there were no paved roads), seemed a dead giveaway.

One evening a few weeks earlier, Joe sat in his office, sipping a Pepsi. He felt too low to go back to his camper, letting the darkening evening control his mood. He was thinking about one couple whose child had been given a diagnosis of an untreatable genetic disease. They had come to get the diagnosis checked by GeneQuestion, hoping the lab would find the doctor's diagnosis wrong. But the gene sequence Joe's lab had found backed up the information the doctor had given them. The little boy was going to die, and soon.

Joe told the couple, "This is the worst news, and I am very, very sorry to give it to you. The only thing you can do is try to make your son's life as easy as possible. Tell him you will always remember him, that he will live on in your memories, and that you will always love him."

The couple was crying, and Joe felt the same way.

The wife asked Joe, "Should my husband get tested to see where the bad gene came from?"

Joe shook his head and said, "The disease is from a classic recessive gene. In other words, it came from both of you."

"What about more children? Should we try again?"

"There's one chance in four the next child will have the same problem, or, put another way, three chances in four that the child will be all right."

They were silent until the husband asked, "If we try again, can GeneQuestion see if the next child is all right?"

Joe nodded and said, "We sometimes do analyses on fetal tissues. It isn't too hard." He paused and then went on. "What you do with the information is up to you. As I said, it is three to one the next child will be okay. It may be a carrier of the recessive gene, as you both are, but it will grow up normally."

The couple then got up, thanked Joe—*for what?* Joe thought—and left.

Joe's office was getting darker as night fell, but Joe didn't feel hungry, just sad. He brushed away some tears, telling himself he really needed to be more detached. He was just the messenger. No, he couldn't do that. It wasn't his nature. That was why this damn job wore him down. And he was supposed to keep on doing it until he retired. Or until he just couldn't take any more. Finally, Joe forced himself to get up and go back to his camper. He wondered, for the hundredth or thousandth time, if having a wife and family of his own would help, would cushion the downs. Maybe, but first he had to find the wife, and the life he'd had with Stacey didn't exactly encourage him to try again.

The divorce and especially its aftermath had left Joe confused and frightened. He had the grievance, but his ex-wife had behaved as though she were the unjustly injured party. Eventually, Joe concluded that justice had nothing to do with her behavior. He realized that she had set her heart on Joe paying her way through med school, and even if her expectations were unreasonable and selfish, he had disappointed them. That meant she was angry— furiously angry—with him.

However, now Joe lived in the camper, sleeping in it or on top of it, depending on the weather, full-time. Officially, his address was at his workplace. No one could bother him at work, no one except the IRS, his subordinates, and most particularly his new GeneQuestion boss.

The new boss was a woman named Hope Dearing, aka "Hopeless"—for even though she had a PhD (the reason she was Joe's boss), she was utterly clueless about the procedures used. She was also too distant to help with unhappy clients or lab workers with problems—or seemingly any other human beings. Joe had not been surprised to learn she was not married either.

She became an object of derision for everyone in the lab, though of course not to her face—at least until Joe realized that in a way, he was treating her the same way his ex-wife and her friends had been treating him. At that point, Joe felt ashamed of his behavior and began making extra efforts to explain what was going on and why. He also gently but persistently tried to get his subordinates not to be disrespectful to her. Joe couldn't be sure how effective his efforts were, but at least his boss was beginning to pick up on the reasons for the lab procedures, why and how they worked.

Now Joe could work on the job he was best suited for—his scholarship. He shook off the memories of mournful conferences with clients and the dealings with his new boss at GeneQuestion. He sat at his computer at work, dealing with two weeks' worth of problems. They were mostly small ones, since Joe had trained his subordinates, and most of the time things went smoothly. He had gone over his solutions to the other things with Hopeless—Dr. Dearing, sorry—and she seemed to understand and even appreciate Joe's efforts. But today had been a very long day.

Now Joe was alone at work, patching, splicing, reorganizing, and occasionally rewriting his dissertation. Despite all the red ink, he made good progress. Feeling a little better, he pulled a can of stew out of his desk, opened it, poured the stew into a bowl, and put it in the microwave everyone shared.

While it was heating, Joe stretched and looked out the window—carefully, since he was still paranoid about being watched. It had been a day of heat that Joe had long come to associate with Nevada in the summer. He wasn't going back to his camper. Even sleeping on top of the thing would be impossible until well into the night.

The microwave signaled that his meal was ready. Joe took the hot stew to his desk, using his handkerchief to carry the bowl, and began to eat cautiously. He saved his changes to the dissertation, backed them up on a thumb drive, and then exited to look at new developments in forensics.

Nothing looked interesting—well, maybe one thing did. There was a new program that would use frontal and side pictures of human skulls, and add "flesh" to show what the person had looked like when alive. This probably wasn't as good as adding a quarter inch of modeling clay all around, but Joe decided he would go to Winnemucca, take pictures of the skull he had gotten the molar from, and put them on the last page of his dissertation. He would show the man clean shaven but with blue eyes and red hair. This would put a human face on his research project. He would give copies to Penny and her boss at the museum. Since this was nondestructive, they would be delighted.

Joe checked his watch, and then Penny's card. He saw what could only be her home number and dialed. She answered, and Joe told her what he wanted to try. As he expected, she was delighted.

Joe told her, "I don't know when I can get away, but I'll call you again. Okay?"

"Sure, Joe. I'll tell my boss. Sounds great." And both disconnected.

Joe downloaded the new forensic program, read it over again carefully, and finished his stew. Then he reached into his drawer for a candy bar. As he ate, he thought he would very much like to get better acquainted with Penny, if she was single and unattached. Unlikely, to be sure, since she was an attractive woman. Still ...

After washing up his bowl and spoon, Joe got back to his dissertation and worked well into the night. He actually finished the thing, backed it up on his computer and on his thumb drive, and then e-mailed it to his adviser at the university. Joe got up, turned off the light, and looked outside. Seeing no one hanging around, he headed for his pickup.

Joe had paid the extra money to park in a big parking deck nearby for the extra security. He walked fast, got into the parking deck without being approached, and found his pickup by itself, looking rather forlorn. Joe saw no problems, no flat tires, and no evidence of dynamite underneath. He didn't feel self-conscious and didn't really think he was being paranoid—just careful. He started the engine, holding his breath, then left the parking deck and headed for what he loosely called "home." Outside, the air temperature had dropped a lot, though not enough to roll down the windows and turn off the air conditioner.

It was past one when Joe got to his camper. He saw no evidence of visitors, so he took off his shoes, put on slippers, and went out into the rapidly cooling desert air, carrying his sleeping bag. He climbed up to the top of the camper, laid the sleeping bag out on its roof, and lay down himself.

His alarm clock woke him at seven. As usual, he very much wanted to sleep longer, but the sun was up, the air temperature was rising rapidly, and he had a full bladder. He got his shoes on, threw the sleeping bag into the camper, locked the door, and headed for work.

In his office, he recovered his electric razor, toothbrush, and toothpaste and went to the men's room. Twenty minutes later, shaved, showered, teeth shined, and bladder emptied, he returned to his office, took a can of Pepsi from his small refrigerator and two candy bars from his desk, and proceeded to undo the work of the toothbrush. By now it was just nine o'clock, time to open the shop.

Over the course of the day, Joe got a call from Penny, who said her boss would be delighted to put a face on the skull, and an e-mail from his dissertation adviser at the university with a few more changes and corrections. After the workday ended, Joe made the requested changes in the dissertation, saved everything, and sent it back. He also asked his adviser at the university when he could defend his dissertation. He didn't mention the facial reconstruction; if it worked, the face would be the last page of the results section—a good, dramatic ending.

As the week passed, Joe got a better idea of when he could go to Winnemucca. He would have to take the afternoon off, explaining to Hope Dearing what he was doing and why. She appeared interested in the idea of the lab's possibly earning a bit extra, doing facial reconstructions for the police. Joe didn't think that was likely, but kept his doubts to himself.

Just before ten on Thursday, Joe headed east for Winnemucca. He was at the museum before noon, was greeted by a smiling Penny, and went to take some pictures. Penny's boss brought out the skull. Joe had a clean handkerchief to set it on, as well as a ruler for scale for the reconstruction. Taking the pictures took just a few minutes: several front face, a few side views. Then it was done. Penny's boss seemed a little disappointed that the procedure was so simple.

Joe told her, "I'll try the reconstruction program tonight. If it works, I'll e-mail both of you a color copy."

Both women eagerly accepted his offer. Then Penny's boss left, taking the skull with her.

Penny told Joe, "I was going to get a local restaurant to send me a loose-meat sub. Do you want one, or did you have other plans?"

If Joe had other plans, he immediately changed them. Reaching into his pocket for his wallet, he asked, "How much?"

Penny replied, "Five should do it. We can eat in my office."

She led the way to a moderately cluttered place, indicated where Joe was to sit, and called the restaurant. She ordered two sandwiches with drinks. Joe raised his eyebrows.

Penny told Joe, "If you can give the woman who delivers these, say, two dollars, that will make us square."

So Joe counted out seven dollars and handed the money to Penny. Then he sat back, enjoying the air-conditioning while attempting to see if Penny was wearing a wedding ring. He was trying to be discreet about it, but Penny immediately noticed.

"No, I'm not married. Divorced. No kids. You?"

Joe replied, "The same."

Then there was a knock at Penny's door, and a heavyset woman appeared with the sandwiches and drinks. The sandwiches, filled with pot roast cooked to fragments, were quite good, Joe thought, and he told Penny so. Penny, her mouth full, nodded. Eventually conversation could resume.

Penny asked Joe, "When do you defend?"

A week from this Friday. If I pass, look to the west for fireworks, colored lights, and drunken yells. If I don't, just the drunken yells."

Joe smiled and Penny smiled back. Then Joe left with his pictures.

Several customers needed stroking, or at least a sympathetic ear, over their test results. Joe tried to give the best advice he could: don't be hasty, try to let the emotional dust settle before taking any major steps, and above all, put the child or children first. If health issues were involved, Joe told the customers that cures or at least successful treatments were an ever-growing possibility. Boilerplate to be sure, but Joe had been through an emotional mill himself, so his sympathy was at least partly real.

There were also technical issues, and Joe had to deal with them while involving Hope Dearing as much as possible. For the emotional part of Joe's job, he was certain Hope was just too detached. By the time six o'clock had rolled around, everything was back on schedule, and Joe's boss and coworkers had left. Joe now began working on the facial reconstruction.

5

FACE FROM THE PAST

The program was not straightforward, and Joe's curses had become very repetitive before he at last noticed an icon he hadn't before. He clicked on it, and the program began to work. Almost magically, the image of the skull began to be covered with cyber-flesh, about a millimeter deep each time, until a recognizable live human face had emerged. Joe clicked on the eye color and hair color and length desired, and there it was: a face like one that could be seen on any street of any town in northwestern Europe. Joe shivered before the gaze of the image. *Who were you?* he thought.

He saved it, backed it up, and made about fifteen color copies, more than enough for his dissertation. Finally, he e-mailed the image to his dissertation adviser and to Penny and her boss. He looked at the time: nearly one—again. He felt the reaction; he was beyond tired. If there had been a couch where he worked, he would have bedded down there. But there wasn't. The floor was linoleum, and he had to drive back.

At dawn, Joe got up from his sleeping bag on top of his camper feeling very rusty indeed. He managed to get back to the lab, varying his routine only by downing two bottles of Pepsi instead of his usual one. This seemed to have no particular effect, and Joe prepared to endure the day.

It was a very busy one, unfortunately. Joe had the feeling the entire time that things were slipping out of his control. They never actually did, but the feeling lasted even past six, when the lab closed. Now he had to modify his dissertation for his talk, struggling to express himself clearly and succinctly. Fortunately, the picture, which to Joe looked haunting, would just be icing on the cake. Penny e-mailed Joe her thoughts, which were much like his. Her boss was going to use the picture in the museum's exhibits, so Joe hoped he would be able to get another tooth for carbon 14 analysis without any opposition.

And now there was another e-mail, this time from Joe's dissertation adviser at the University of Nevada:

> Joe, just saw the facial reconstruction. Don't bother putting it in your dissertation. It might go in the paper, but the carbon 14 date, definitely. One of the guys on your committee can do that. Just get another tooth. Cheers, FL.

Joe smiled: FL was Hersh's term for himself and meant "Fearless Leader." Then Joe realized he didn't need to write any more, at least for the next few days, and could go home. He looked at the clock: seven thirty. He could go to sleep early tonight if it had cooled down enough. He did make sure the picture was included in his PowerPoint slides, just before the acknowledgments, saved and backed up everything, shut down, and got up to leave. He looked around, and then out of habit checked outside for any people hanging around. Seeing none, he headed for his pickup. He decided he would get a pizza—large, with thin crust. He was really feeling like celebrating.

On the drive to his camper, the face kept coming back, dampening his happiness. This was foolish: he really didn't know why the Paiutes had massacred all those people. Perhaps they had good reason, perhaps not, but the face haunted him more and more.

He assured the face, "By publishing what I have found, in a sense I will bring you to life again. I will tell your story to the entire world."

The following Sunday, since it had rained for three straight days, there was water flowing in Gold Creek. That in itself was remarkable in this part of Nevada in the summer. Joe had bought a gold pan a year or so back, but hadn't used it yet. Today he would see if he could make some money. He took the gold pan and a shovel out to the creek.

Joe had never panned for gold, but he knew what the theory was. And looking at the creek, he figured gold particles would probably settle just past two big rocks. These rocks diverted the flow, slowing it down, so Joe began shoveling sediment downstream of them into his pan, dipping the pan into the cool, flowing water, then swirling the sediment to spill the lighter material out.

So much for theory. It was hard work, hard physical work, and Joe wasn't used to that. He took frequent breaks and then finally had reduced his first panful quite a bit. He looked carefully at the remainder and saw that, yes, there were flakes, bits, even a very small yellow pebble. Yes, yes, there was gold here!

Excited, Joe went into his camper to get something to put the flakes and pebble—it seemed too small to call it a nugget—into. He could find only a drinking glass. It wasn't very clean, so he rinsed it out in the creek. He continued to add water to the pan and swirl the diminishing residue until only yellowish stuff was left. At this point, Joe realized he had to transfer the gold into the glass, and that was impossible. He needed an eyedropper or something like that, and he didn't have one.

After thinking some, Joe added two more shovelfuls of sediment and continued. Despite the excitement of having some real gold in his pan, he seemed to wear out even faster. He guessed he was becoming more efficient, but it was a very slow process.

However, the amount of golden residue was distinctly greater. At this point, Joe decided to get something to eat and to get some small bottles or jars as well as something with which to transfer the gold into them. He set the pan in his truck (he wasn't going to leave it in the camper) and drove to the University of Nevada.

The building where Joe had worked was open, and people were coming and going despite it being Sunday. Joe went to one of the neighboring labs and got two or three scintillation vials. He also rummaged in the trash cans, found two 10-milliliter plastic disposable pipettes, rinsed them out in deionized water, shook them dry, and was about to leave when he realized he was going to have to weigh his find.

He weighed the scintillation vials and marked their weights on their sides with a marker. Now he could get a pizza and large drink. Panning gold was much harder work than it seemed.

Back at his place, he ate and drank, then had enough energy—only just, it seemed—to pan two more shovelfuls. He dug deeper and was rewarded with the shine of three actual pea-sized nuggets. The amount of dust was greater as well. He spent the last hour or so of daylight transferring his catch to one of the vials, except for the nuggets, which he transferred with his fingers. He was delighted to find he had too much gold for one vial and had to use two. Now he would have to dry the gold and weigh it.

The next morning Joe drove to work, stopping to pick up something at McDonald's. At work, he shaved, brushed his teeth, emptied bowels and bladder, and washed his hands and face. Mondays were fairly busy (Saturdays were the busiest), and Joe dealt with clients, dispensing sympathy where called for, genuine sympathy, for Joe knew all too well what it felt like to be betrayed by someone you loved and trusted.

Toward noon, Joe checked the supplies of chemicals, noted three that were getting low, and filled out an order form. He had to take the form to Hope Dearing for endorsement. He was expecting an argument and was not disappointed.

"Joe, I just ordered some of these."

"We're doing a lot of business. I don't think we have more than a week's supply of two of these left, and getting the third always seems to take extra time. And"—Joe leaned forward to emphasize this point—"if we run out of any of them, we have to close the business."

Joe stared her right in the eyes, and after a moment, she initialed the order. Joe nodded, left with the order, and saw it phoned in.

He talked with the staff, looked at the instruments, noted they were all working well (Joe was careful to keep everything serviced and running), and went back to extract a can of soup from his desk. He opened it, heated the soup in a dish in the microwave, and ate the stuff while standing up. After this repast, he began to meet with more customers. It took the rest of the afternoon and was very wearing emotionally. Also, the effect on Joe's muscles of the gold panning Sunday was really beginning to intensify.

After the lab closed at six, Joe removed the caps from the two glass scintillation vials, set them in the microwave, set the thing on low heat for five minutes, and started it. Then he took a couple of candy bars out of his desk along with a canned drink out of his small refrigerator and began rereading his dissertation. Every few minutes Joe would stop reading, check the scintillation vials, and then give them more time: first ten minutes, then twenty-five. The levels of water in the vials dropped, disappearing below the level of gold dust. Joe began to recap and shake the vials between microwaving.

His reading of his dissertation otherwise went on steadily, stopped only by occasional typos. Joe marked them with paper clips. About ten, he realized he was fading. He got up, surprised by how stiff he was becoming, and put his dissertation away. Then he checked the vials once more. The gold seemed dry, so Joe weighed the two vials, wrote down the weights, subtracted the tare weights, and added the weights of the gold in the two vials. In grams, it was a sizeable amount. But gold prices were per ounce; was that the Troy ounce or the other? Joe shook his head; he really needed to sleep.

The next morning, Joe couldn't believe how stiff and sore he was. He tried to stretch his muscles, but felt nothing but pain. He locked his camper, got in his pickup, and headed for work. He got out of his truck to buy some breakfast, hoping the extra movement required would help. Then he went through his usual morning routine. But that didn't help either.

There were fewer customers that day, but they seemed to take more time. One of the pizza places, Round Table, was having a special on large one-topping pizzas. Joe ordered one, thin crust, with pepperoni for his lunch and dinner. It arrived, but Joe found himself sharing it with Hope Dearing. She was talking about pricing of services, so they finished the pizza together. Hope noticed Joe's discomfort, and he told her he had been doing some digging at his place on Sunday. When Hope asked, Joe told her roughly where and how he lived. He added that he was hoping to build once he had enough money.

The afternoon was very quiet. Joe was able to figure how much the gold he had was worth: about $8,000. Having a specific value given was bound to be a little disappointing until Joe reminded himself that (a) he had gotten that in just one day, a very long day but only a day, and (b) there was certainly much, much more in the creek bed. Building his house was looking more and more possible. Joe decided to start calling house designers. At least once he had decided exactly what he wanted built.

Now there was more reading of his dissertation. More paper clips too. Joe decided to knock off early—early for him, that is: nine. He got another hamburger and large drink and drove home. When he got there, he sat on the steps of his camper, looking at the lot, trying to imagine a house here. Joe sat, drank, and thought. Finally he decided on a two-story place, with a cathedral living room, big fans in the ceiling, and solar panels on the roof, three or four bedrooms on the second floor, and two or maybe three bathrooms. Suddenly Joe remembered: where in hell was the water supposed to come from? Drilling a well would have to come first. Aside from that, balconies at each end of the second floor, so Joe could sit or sleep with the lights of Carson City in the distance or else the quiet hills and mountains to the southeast. Perhaps a garage. Joe stretched, undressed, and took his sleeping bag up to the top of the camper. As he lay down under the stars, he wondered if Penny would be willing to live here with him ...

Joe's sleep was disturbed, partly because his muscles were sore but now once more by his memories of the skull. Cyber-fleshed, it was in a way more unsettling: it seemed to be trying to talk to Joe. It had things to say, and Joe was trying to understand what they were ...

LOOKING FOR ANSWERS

The GeneQuestion lab where Joe worked had a small separate restroom with an even smaller shower. Rather than have to rent a room somewhere periodically, Joe used it. So on Friday, after the usual derisory meal, Joe showered, reshaved, brushed his teeth once more, and put on a suit and a tie as well, in preparation for his defense. He met clients, checked operations, and touched bases with everyone, including Hope Dearing, until three. Things were quiet then, so Joe got the three bottles of California sparkling wine he hoped to celebrate with, walked to his truck, and drove north to Reno. He was at the university about fifteen minutes early. He took his presentation and a bag with the three bottles in with him.

The auditorium had a scattering of people, including his committee ... and there was Penny. Joe thought his jaw would drop off his face.

"If I had known you were coming, I would have worn a tux."

"Do you own a tux?"

"For you, one with a cane and a top hat."

They both laughed.

Joe saw everyone looking at the two of them and realized

he had to set up. So after a smiling nod to Penny, he went to the podium and did just that. Things were certainly starting well. Joe waited until his FL introduced him and gave a censored account of his background. Then it was up to Joe.

Joe described the legends and the findings at Lovelock in the early 1900s, and showed some of the newspaper pictures. Then he spoke of his interest in the topic and outlined the current methods of analysis of old DNA. He thought he was presenting the facts clearly, and answered the few questions, such as how old the sample that Joe analyzed was. Then he presented his results and conclusions—all perfectly straightforward. The major question was of course, "How old is the sample?" Joe was again straightforward in his reply. He needed more material, and was negotiating to get some. He didn't look at Penny as he said this. Finally, Joe showed the reconstructed face. He thought the audience was totally mesmerized. Then came the acknowledgments, including Penny and Penny's boss, and it was over.

There was applause. Everyone was smiling. Joe returned the slide to the reconstructed face and, on impulse, saluted it. Several people shook his hand. His committee gathered around the podium, and after looking at one another and nodding, his adviser pulled some sheets of paper out and everyone signed. No meeting afterward was necessary. Joe had his doctorate.

Joe reached down and pulled the three bottles of bubbly out, then realized he didn't have a corkscrew or glasses. One of his committee members suggested knocking the tops off the bottles and everyone drinking directly from them. However, his adviser had a fancy knife with a corkscrew along with about a dozen other utensils and began to open a bottle. And another committee member ran up the steps of the auditorium and then returned a few minutes later with an opened box containing plastic champagne glasses.

Everyone took a glass, including Penny. Joe poured her glass first, then those of his committee members, and finally one for himself. Once more, Joe turned to the face on the screen and drank a toast to it.

At this point, Penny told Joe, "I brought another tooth for the carbon dating."

Everyone looked at her as she opened her big purse and pulled a small glass jar out. Inside was a molar that rattled as she moved the jar. Joe could see that the jar had once held horseradish sauce, but it looked clean.

As if in response to Joe's thought, Penny said, "I washed it out first. I hope that is enough."

Joe looked at one member of his committee, a man who did carbon 14 dating. The man smiled and took the jar from Joe.

"This is about as good as you can do. I will get a date on it and report back"—he nodded to Joe—"within a few days."

Everyone drank to that, and then Joe's committee members put their glasses down, each saying he had to drive home. After one last round of handshakes and waves, they left, leaving Joe and Penny alone together.

Joe was quite overcome by emotion now, and began to talk.

"Penny, thank you so much for coming here on my special day. Your being here made it much more special."

Joe opened his mouth to say more and then decided anything more would probably embarrass them both, so he just smiled.

Penny smiled, too. Joe could see she was quite moved, though she opted for a light touch: "Just for a tooth?"

"The tooth will be very important to"—here Joe gestured at the slide, still on the screen—"but just having you here …"

Joe once more couldn't think of anything else to say that wouldn't be repetitive or presumptuous or both, so he bent down and brought up the unopened third bottle of sparkling wine. He laid it in her arms with ceremony, trying for a lighter touch.

"Try not to drink it all on the way back."

This made them both laugh. Then Penny kissed Joe on the cheek and Joe took one of her hands and kissed it. Then with a final smile, she left.

Joe looked up at the face—was it smiling?—raised his glass once more to it, drank the last few sips, and went to shut off the projector after exiting his PowerPoint and pulling out the thumb drive. Joe took everything, being especially careful with the precious signed pieces of paper, out to the parking lot. He couldn't see any problems, so he started the pickup without cringing much. He went to a "full-service" copy shop. It was a little expensive, but Joe wanted to get his dissertation corrected, copied, and bound starting this afternoon. And checking his watch, he saw it was still afternoon, though he felt much older. Joe had his original dissertation with the paper clips. He got a computer and his dissertation CD, corrected everything he had found, backed it up on a thumb drive, and gave the CD to a girl behind the counter.

"I think ten copies, bound. Here are the signed papers that go in front. When can you have them?"

"Tuesday," the girl told Joe. "Do you want a dedication page?"

Joe thought about it. The dissertation was dedicated to his parents and to his professor at the university. He decided to add a line: "To Penny Echeverria: for everything." Joe paid for the copying and binding using his credit card, and left.

It was starting to get a little dark. Though Joe hadn't drunk much champagne, he was still flying a little. And it was too hot to bed down. He would get something to eat, something decent, and he headed for a popular Mexican restaurant. There was, Joe hoped, good parking lot security .... Joe wished he had a place of his own so he could invite people—no, there was only one person he wanted to invite—to stay over, to stay always. He would have to get started on his house.

As he drove to the restaurant, he automatically looked to see if someone was following, but he saw no one. His thoughts turned once again to the face.

"Soon," Joe promised it, "soon I will be able to tell your story."

HOUSE ON GOLD CREEK

The cost of the divorce had left Joe nearly broke, so he had had to finance his truck, the lot, even the camper. By now he had paid off these loans, but to build a house, he would need a mortgage. However, the mortgage company would insist on an address for the house, and Joe wanted as few people as possible to know where he lived. That meant he would have to save for years to pay to build, or ....

Joe was a fast eater, and as was always the case, he was alone. When he came out of the restaurant, there was still plenty of daylight left. He drove back to his place. On the way it occurred to him that if he needed money to drill a well, design a house, and build it (and he certainly did), he had better use the long evenings to pan a lot more gold. So he parked his pickup, took the pan and shovel out. He kept these concealed so he wouldn't give away the fact that Gold Creek in fact had gold in it, and went to the creek.

The flow of water was dropping, no question. Joe took two shovelfuls of sediment, added water, and began swirling. He was definitely getting better at panning, but the light was going fast. Still, he could see nuggets and dust in the twilight. He would finish in the morning, Saturday. It was his lab's busiest day, so Joe set his alarm for 6:30 a.m., got his sleeping bag out of the camper, and climbed onto its top.

Saturday was even busier than usual because there were several clients left over from Friday. This surprised Joe, and he had to repeatedly apologize and explain his absence the day before. He was his tactful, conciliatory, and sympathetic best, but it took the entire morning to catch up. Taking a lunch break was impossible. Joe wished yet again that Hope Dearing could do something more than sit in her office—*doing what?* Joe wondered. Finally the lab closed, and Joe decided to pan gold rather than begin the paper based on his dissertation. The paper could wait; the water in the creek wouldn't.

Joe got another combo at a fast-food place and drove back. This time he had a few hours of daylight left, and did four shovelfuls. The creek was definitely going dry; this week would see the end of the panning. On the other hand, the yields were still good.

On Sunday, Joe processed shovelful after shovelful. The gold accumulated. By evening, he couldn't really do any more panning and went to sleep, figuring he had at least two or three times the gold he had collected before. But he would have to dry it and weigh it. He decided he needed a Mason jar to hold it all.

He used Monday evening to pan for gold again. The water flow had almost stopped, and Joe decided this would be the last day. Aside from the dwindling water supply, he was very sore once again and knew he'd feel that way even tomorrow and Wednesday.

He should hear about the carbon 14 dating this week, which would give him an excuse to call Penny again. He didn't really know what date he wanted. From the description of the finding of the remains, he was fairly confident the date would be in the hundreds of years ago: there had been some four feet of dust and bat droppings above the remains, and that wouldn't have accumulated in a short time. Once he had the date, he would have to write the paper. His professor at the university had suggested he try having it published in the *Journal of Applied Genetics*. Among his many other tasks, Joe would have to look up their format. He wondered if they did color figures.

He would have to dry the gold. And weigh it. And, oh yes, call architects to get someone on board to plan his house and supervise its building. But that brought him back to money.

On Tuesday Joe hunched his way through the day's work. His coworkers expressed their concern. Was he sick? Injured? Joe simply said he was working out and that it had left him stiff and sore. He couldn't tell anyone what he had really been doing or he'd have a horde of uninvited guests on his property.

About five that afternoon, Joe got a call from the man on his committee who had volunteered to get a carbon 14 date from the molar Penny had brought over.

"Making all sorts of assumptions, such as lack of seafood in the diet, which seems okay in view of the location, the owner of the skull died 1,220 years ago, plus or minus 150 years," he said. "And you can quote me."

Joe wrote the numbers down and replied, "So time of death was about 780 CE, give or take a century and a half. As far as quoting you—how about your name as an author?"

"I wouldn't say no to that. My CV this year has been a bit on the thin side. But what does Hersh say?"

"I'll ask him, but I suspect he'll go along. For the usual consideration."

The man laughed and said, "Go ahead. Let me know what he says. You can edit out the cuss words."

"That won't leave much, but I'll do that."

Both men laughed, and Joe hung up.

Then Joe dialed Penny on his cell phone. To his delight, she answered.

"Hi, Joe. Did you get the carbon 14 date?"

"Just now. The skull is 1,220 plus or minus 150 years old, and you can tell your boss."

"Wow. Definitely pre-Columbian. Okay, we'll put that in the exhibition. Where will this be published?"

"Hoping standards have fallen sufficiently, the *Journal of Applied Genetics*."

Penny laughed. "Will you start writing now?"

Joe sighed. "Yes. And I am also going to hire some architects to have a house built, a place where I can actually sleep indoors, a place to live. Given money, I mean."

"Will you have enough?"

"I'll just have to see. Eventually, yes. The gold-plated water faucets may have to go, at least the outside ones."

"This place is beginning to sound interesting."

"Good. I will do my best to make it so."

Both laughed, and the conversation ended.

That brought the gold to mind, so Joe began drying what he had recently panned. While this was going on, he began looking up architects in the phone directory. Since he didn't know how much money he had and would need, all he could see was that there were quite a few architects and builders listed.

Joe stirred the gold, breaking up the caked lumps, reset the timer on the microwave, and began looking for a Mason jar. He eventually found one in a drawer full of odds and ends used for meals, weighed it, and wrote the weight on the side of the jar with a marker. Then he called up the site of the *Journal of Applied Genetics*. He noted that they did not publish color plates for less than a small fortune, and decided to print out a copy of their directions for submission of manuscripts

Two cycles on the microwave later, the gold was dry. Joe very carefully scooped, swept, and poured it into the Mason jar. He added his original take and weighed the total. It felt heavy. Joe calculated he had more than $120,000 worth. He should certainly be able to get a plan and make a start. He was in business. Now he really should get started on the paper, but Joe was too excited to settle down enough. He compromised by printing out the carbon 14 procedures and data and conclusions that had just come in.

He told himself he needed nourishment and needed to wind down so he could sleep. He got up, turned out the lights, looked carefully out the windows for anybody hanging around, and then left. He moved fast, carrying his Mason jar in his briefcase, and got to his truck without seeing anyone.

During a spare moment on Friday afternoon, Joe looked up gold buyers in the Yellow Pages. One outfit, Bonanzas Unlimited, bought "raw" gold. They were open late on Fridays. So that Friday, Joe managed to finish and clear out early—for him. The place was on the outskirts of Carson City. It was built like a fort, with plenty of security. No, the place was more like a prison: gray concrete-block walls, walls that looked thick and *felt* thick, big concrete barriers around the building so no one could bulldoze their way inside, and even coils of razor wire around the edges of the roof. In the back was a big brick chimney with currents of hot air coming from the top. The door was heavy, double glass covered with a steel screen. Joe went inside.

A man ahead of him—middle-aged, overweight—was selling a gold nugget the size of Joe's thumb. He was telling the man behind the counter, a lean, grizzled man carrying a six-shooter in a holster, "My dad won this in a card game thirty-odd years ago. Now he's gone, I figured I would sell it."

The man behind the counter nodded, took the nugget, placed it in some sort of instrument, and turned the instrument on. Evidently the nugget was indeed gold, so the man weighed it and punched some buttons, and a printer produced a check along with a statement showing how the total on the check had been determined. The customer looked at the check, appeared to be pleased, and left, tossing the statement into a trash can. The man behind the counter looked at Joe, who produced the Mason jar, which was nearly full of dust and small gold pieces. The man poured Joe's gold into a container and went through the same procedure. The check he handed Joe was for a little over $102,000, and made out to "bearer." Joe saw the check was drawn on an account in the Bank of America, where Joe banked as well. Joe took the check and statement. He noticed that the man buying the gold hadn't asked for his ID or Social Security number. Two more customers appeared.

Joe went to a branch of the Bank of America that stayed open late on Fridays. While he was in line, he looked at the statement. It said Joe had sold "old gold." The outfit that had bought it had taken 20 percent as the cost of refining plus profit. Joe filled out a deposit slip and gave it and the check to the woman behind the counter. She deposited the check without batting an eye and gave Joe the receipt.

Joe asked, "When will the money be available?"

The woman looked at the screen in front of her and said, "It is now."

Joe went back to his truck, feeling a little overwhelmed. He couldn't believe how lucky he had been this time. But considering his experience with Stacey, he supposed it all evened out. Now Joe needed to start being careful as hell—careful in spending the money. He had enough money now to at least build the shell of a house, and there was almost certainly more gold to be panned, given enough water. So Joe went to get his usual Supreme pizza with a large Pepsi and then drove back to his camper, always keeping an eye out for people following him. While he drove, it occurred to Joe that the reason why the man who bought the gold hadn't asked for ID—at least Joe's ID—was that he must have figured Joe didn't want anyone else, *anyone* else, knowing Joe panned a lot of gold dust. If word got out, Joe would have a lot of unwanted company. Otherwise, the money Joe had made was between Joe's conscience and the IRS. And Joe wasn't sure he could completely trust everyone in the IRS. The people peddling estate jewelry, assuming they hadn't stolen it, probably didn't owe any taxes on Mama's gold bracelet. But again, that was their concern. Still, what if what was sold was stolen? Presumably the owner figured he could size up his customers.

That evening Joe called several builders. Some were busy, and some didn't do individual residences, and Joe finally decided to ask everyone at GeneQuestion who they had heard was a good builder. Eventually Joe talked to someone who knew someone who knew someone who was having a house built. The man was very positive about his builders, a husband-and-wife team. Given the size and location of the house, their price was reasonable. The man had the names of two other people who had used these builders and gave Joe their phone numbers. Both were very positive as well. One said, "Their name is Russell, Jim and Estelle. They design and build. They do it all. You can trust them." Also, the builders were finishing up their current project. So Joe called them.

They agreed to come out to Joe's lot the next Sunday. Joe gave them the directions but wound up telling them he would meet them at the parking garage outside GeneQuestion at 10:00 a.m. Joe decided that since this outfit wanted Joe's his business, they would get it.

That Sunday morning, Joe met the builder/ architects as arranged and led them out to his lot. They walked around it and talked briefly to each other, and then the husband turned to Joe.

"Right here is the best site," he said. "A well will have to be drilled first. We take it the creek is usually dry?"

"Yes," Joe said. "I was thinking of a cathedral ceiling, three bedrooms and a bath on the second floor to the rear of the living room, a Franklin stove in the middle of the living room, and a second bath on the ground floor. Not sure about a garage. I would really like to make the house solar electric, with panels covering the roof."

The man said, "Look, solar panels just won't give you enough energy, at least when you need it. We recommend a gas-powered generator that will come on when needed and cut off when not. So you don't want the living room entirely ringed by bedrooms?"

Joe thought a moment and then said, "No. Not on the front side of the house."

The man looked toward Joe's camper. "You live here?"

"In winter. Summers I sleep on the roof."

The woman said, "It would be helpful if we could use it during the day. Is that possible?"

Joe shrugged and told them, "I'll just move my stuff to clear as much space as possible."

Joe then showed them the inside of the camper.

The couple nodded, and the man said, "We'll do this on a cost-plus basis with payments every Friday. That will assure that the subcontractors arrive on schedule. My guess is about a hundred thousand, give or take, depending on your choice of materials."

Joe stood there, thinking. He had sold his gold for more than $102,000, so he should have enough. He began to feel excited: a place of his own at last, maybe a place he could bring someone .... Joe nodded and shook hands with the couple. They seemed pleased too—maybe they needed the business. Well, fine.

The man said, "We'll bring you the plans and a contract next week."

Things were really moving now, Joe thought, and he nodded agreement.

After the couple left, Joe sniffed the desert air. Then he got back in his truck and went to his office to work some more on the paper. He was using big chunks of his dissertation, suitably trimmed, and conservatively estimated he was half through. As he worked, he wondered if he could write a magazine or newspaper article with Penny. Sunday supplements used color, no problem. And working on a project with Penny was something he really wanted to do.

As if his thoughts had connected with hers, Joe saw a message from her on his e-mail asking how his meeting with the architects had gone. Joe had discussed plans for the house with her, so replied to her:

> I think I have builder-architects. They guessed 100K, more or less, though my guess is it will be more. They will get back with me next week, they said. And how was your day?

Penny replied:

> Went to church. Thought about things. How is your
> paper coming?

Joe told her, and she replied:

> I will sign off now. Let me know how the meeting
> with the builders goes.

He replied:

> Will do.

Monday was very wearing. Joe had to tell four men that the child that was supposedly theirs wasn't. Over the years, Joe had gone from trying to stay out of these meetings to detachment—the way doctors were supposed to be—to trying to be sympathetic to being fully emotionally involved. He really could and did feel their pain. He tried to counsel them, but knew it was a waste of time. Each man would have to work out his own problems. Somehow the good news he was able to give most of them wasn't nearly enough to compensate for the bad news he had to give the rest. At least he managed to finish the rough draft of his paper.

The GeneQuestion building was in Carson City, the state capital, rather than in nearby Reno or Sparks, which together made up the main transportation center for northern Nevada. Reno-Sparks also had about five times the population of Carson City. Joe eventually guessed that the GeneQuestion building was in Carson City because it was handy to Reno-Sparks but far enough away that the clients wouldn't draw as much attention to themselves.

On Tuesday the builders called and suggested meeting at a Pizza Hut. After some discussion, the three of them agreed upon a time. Otherwise, it was another wearing day. Often the cuckolded husbands were enraged, to the point of being homicidal, although Joe had also seen grown men break down in tears. Joe could only offer sympathy—sympathy that had become more intense over the years—and advice if that was desired—but either way, it was depressing. Joe told himself over and over that he was seeing only a small fraction of the population and that most wives were honest with their husbands. Joe eventually got to the Pizza Hut in a very down mood.

The builders were there, in a booth. The man waved to Joe. Joe was actually reassured that they'd chosen someplace like Pizza Hut, since he knew that one way or another, he would be paying the tab for everyone. Joe sat down in the booth. He was facing the door.

The man showed Joe the plans, which looked okay. Then Joe remembered the balconies—one at each end of the upper-floor hallway in front of the bedrooms and upstairs bathroom. He apologized for forgetting them, but the man grinned and pulled out a different floor plan, which included the two balconies.

Joe laughed and said, "You folks are mind-readers."

"Give the credit to Estelle here," the man said, nodding toward his wife. "She thought it would be a good idea. These will be supported by steel pipes, like the second floor itself. The pipes will be anchored in concrete, so this should be a damn strong house."

Joe nodded approval, and then their waitress appeared. Joe ordered, yet again, a Supreme, thin crust. He knew pizza purists claimed that more than three toppings was a waste—supposedly the tastes of more than that canceled one another out—but Joe liked Supremes. The waitress went to get their drinks, and Joe began looking carefully over the plans. Everything appeared to be there. Having actual drawings seemed to bring the house—his house, his home—alive. There was also a schedule of construction. Evidently, absent any tornados, earthquakes, or other acts of God, his builders were figuring six weeks' construction time, including Saturdays.

Joe was very impressed and said so. "Let's go with these," he added.

Everyone nodded. Their drinks appeared. Joe sat back, drinking his Pepsi. The door to the Pizza Hut opened, and in came one of his cuckolded clients along with a woman that Joe thought was nervous. Joe assumed she was his wife. There was also a girl, about eight years old, looking anxiously at the man who, Joe guessed, she believed was her father. The little girl put a placating hand on the client's arm. The man looked down at her, their eyes met and Joe could see the client's face soften. The client smiled briefly, and the girl smiled back. The three of them went into a back corner booth. Joe was touched and mildly reassured. Maybe things would work out. For the girl's sake, he hoped so.

The pizzas came. Joe began eating. He had ordered a medium and was figuring on eating it all in one sitting. About halfway through the meal, his builder got down to business.

"We will need a down payment—say, fifteen thousand—before we can start."

Joe nodded, and got out his checkbook. He wrote the check, handed it to the man, and said, "Don't spend it all in one place."

The three of them laughed, and the man wrote Joe a receipt. Then he said, "Are you sure we can use your camper during the day? It would be convenient for us to have a place to sit and work while the construction is going on. Otherwise we'll have to rent a camper of our own."

Joe shrugged, swallowed, and replied, "No problem. I've already moved most of my stuff to the bunk at the front end. Like I told you, I don't use the place much, except for storing my things."

The man and his wife nodded. Everyone went back to eating their pizzas. The builders insisted on picking up the tab.

"When will you start?" Joe asked.

The man looked at his wife and then back at Joe. "Expect us at seven tomorrow morning."

Joe usually got up at seven, so he nodded. He shook hands with his builders, and everyone got up to leave.

"See you tomorrow," Joe said in the parking lot. He got into his truck and headed out to his lot. He did not look back at the GeneQuestion client and his family.

When Joe got to his lot, he went into the camper. Remembering his promises to the builders, he moved boxes of books closer to the bunk where he slept in bad weather. He cleared the floor as much as he could and swept out the dirt and sand tracked in over the years he had been staying there.

He couldn't think of the place as his home—just somewhere he could sleep out of the rain. Joe moved through the corridor of boxes of books and clothes and slumped onto the lower bunk. The upper bunk was piled with more boxes. Joe was tired. The day had been cooled by thundershowers, and the inside of the camper was cool too. Outside it was wet and now actually a little cold. So Joe set his alarm clock, took off his shoes, emptied his pockets, and—remembering his ex's antics—got up to latch the door. Then he padded back to the bunk and lay down, though it wasn't full dark yet.

PENNY

Joe woke up. Trucks, big ones, were arriving. His alarm went off, and he got up, refilled his pockets, put on his shoes, and started toward the door just as someone began knocking on it. Joe opened the door to see his builders, plans in hand, along with briefcases.

"I moved my stuff. Disinfection had to wait."

The builders laughed, then came in and looked around. They seemed relieved.

"This will be fine," the man said.

Joe looked out the windows and turned toward the builders. Estelle answered Joe's unasked question.

"Well-drilling rig and a bulldozer."

Joe was pleased.

"Well, I'll be on my way if you don't need me."

They didn't, and Joe got into his truck and drove back into Carson City, where there was a bathroom, a shower, and something to eat.

The day went much better: no unhappy clients. In fact, it was just the opposite. The morning passed quickly. Joe ordered more supplies after checking the inventory. Hope Dearing seemed more willing to trust Joe's judgment, so he didn't have any problems there either. At noon, Joe heated a can of soup in the microwave. He had begun buying croissants instead of bread because he liked their flakiness. He cut two of them in half, toasted them, buttered them, and ate. He began to feel much better.

The afternoon's clients were all pleased with their results too. Then Joe got an e-mail from his professor at the University of Nevada. As the dissertation adviser, he wanted a few changes, all minor. Joe was feeling very excited—so much so, he had trouble making the changes at first. He forced himself to calm down, relax, and think of other things—well, one thing: Penny—before he got back to work. It took him about fifteen minutes to make the changes, and then Joe sent the revised manuscript to the journal. He got a receipt, with a number, almost immediately. Joe heaved a big sigh of relief: his paper was on its way.

By now it was after six, so after his usual look around, Joe left. He picked up a burger and headed for his lot. He was curious. When he got there, he could see that the well drilling had begun and the lot had been cleared and staked. As he expected, the ground was mostly rock, but the bulldozer had done what it could. There were even some wooden forms for concrete taking shape. A good day, Joe thought as he sat down on the steps of his camper and began to eat.

The next day, more cars and trucks showed up. Joe waved to the builders and carefully drove out through the parked pickups. The day was going to be a long one, with lots of clients, which meant giving more bad news. There were problems with some of the instruments too, which meant calling in for repairs once he had persuaded Hope to authorize payment for them. All very vexing.

Just another day at the lab, Joe told himself. Then he got an e-mail from Penny:

Joe, did the builders start yet?

Joe replied:

Yes, the next day. They seem to be hungry, which is the way I like them. They asked to use my camper for an office. I warned them about the need for sterile measures, working there.

To protect you?

No.

How long will they take?

Six weeks, thirty-six working days, starting yesterday.

Did you get your paper off?

Yes.

How long on that?

Depends on the referees. It might be a few weeks, it might be months. Say, Penny, I want to publish that reconstructed face in color somewhere, maybe a Sunday supplement. Can you join me in researching this business? Specifically, aside from the skeletons, is there any record of clothing, personal effects, and tools? There must have been tools. Do you have any contact with the Bureau of Land Management at Lovelock? This is for a share of the fame, of course.

I will check things out. Aside from the pre-Columbian bit, what am I looking for?

Where in hell did they come from?

Okay, I will get on this.

The rest of the day was a scramble. In addition to clients, incoming and outgoing, Joe had to help with emergency repairs to two instruments, show a local repairman one of the other instruments, listen to one of the techs who had personal problems, try to cheer her up, try to cheer himself up, and stay on till past seven when the local repairman told Joe the instrument he had been working on was back in operation. Joe had a payment form signed by Hope Dearing ready and gave it to the man, getting his invoice in exchange. Then the repairman left and Joe could go back to his camper after his usual look around.

Every day at the building site, Joe could see progress. After a week, he wrote another check for $15,000. The well was done—it had a good flow and wasn't too deep—so the builders had a concrete platform made that would hold the power generator for the pump and a tank for water. They would order them. Joe also agreed they would order the refrigerator, dishwasher, clothes washer, dryer, and stove. They said they would get a 20 percent builder's discount, and Joe was coming to trust them. In fact, every day when Joe came back, he was cheered by the progress. The foundation was in, for the steel pipes as well as the walls, and truckloads of lumber were stacked close by. Soon the walls would go up, and then the roof.

At work, Joe got an e-mail from the management. It congratulated Joe on getting his PhD but then asked for his confidential opinion about his boss, Hope Dearing. What did Joe think of her competence, managerial style, and contribution to the company? Two or three years ago, Joe's answers would have been, "what competence?," "very little," and "what contribution?" Now he and Dearing had come to a truce, and in fact, Joe was beginning to like the woman. She was hard to get to know, that was all. So Joe praised her on all counts. He added that the smooth operation of this branch of the company had been achieved and maintained on her watch, and she deserved the credit. Joe sent the e-mail. He was a little worried, but clients were coming in. He really didn't want to have to break in a new boss.

Joe and Penny exchanged e-mails every two or three days. Penny had gone to the original newspaper accounts, and kept Joe up to date on them. Joe learned that Penny had been a history major at Reno, but she had been there when Joe was married. Joe called the local paper and talked to the editor of the Sunday supplement. The woman seemed interested in running the story.

That afternoon, Joe got another e-mail from Penny:

> Joe, heard about your paper yet? I may be on to something here.

He replied:

> No, but it's a little soon. I talked with the editor of the Sunday supplement here, and she was interested. What do you have?

> The bodies were well preserved, including the clothes. The newspapers said the clothes were some sort of cloth, with a tartan pattern.

> Tartan? As in Scots?

> Yes.

> What about weapons? Tools?

> Pretty much rusted away, which means iron. There were duck calls and duck decoys, one of them with feathers on it. And some inscribed stones, which seem to have vanished. Oh, and there was a gold button or ornament, with a picture of a fat little man, cross-legged.

> Doesn't sound Scottish to me.

> No. It rings a bell, but that is all it's doing.

Well, I see clients coming in. Let me know what you think it means.

Right.

Joe went out to talk to the next of what seemed to be many clients for the late afternoon. It was well past six when he finished, and everyone else had gone home. Everyone except Hope Dearing, that is. She was sitting at her desk waiting for a call, Joe guessed. She was all dressed up, Joe could smell her perfume out in the hall, and she seemed nervous. Joe paused before her door and waved. She looked up at Joe.

Joe was struck, for the first time, by how—not attractive, but how *not unattractive* she could be. She was middle sized, like Joe himself, and had a good figure, but her best feature was her eyes, which were large and gray, maybe a bit overly mascaraed, but still very nice. She just nodded at Joe in her vague way, and Joe went on out. He got his usual burger and drove to the site.

The walls were going up fast. Part of the first floor had been started. In a couple of days, the roof would be on, just the plywood over the rafters, but Joe was looking forward to it. There was a note from his builders asking for another $20,000. Joe wrote the check, put it in an envelope on the small tabletop in his camper they used as a desk, sat down, and ate. He could see the metal flanges welded to the pipes that would help hold up the second floor as well as the roof. Everything looked very solid. Joe got up, grabbed his sleeping bag, and climbed the ladder onto the roof of the camper. He realized he had forgotten his alarm clock but knew the builders and their people would wake him up in time.

As Joe began to drift off, it occurred to him that he was getting a little old to be living this way. When he had begun to sleep on the roof of the camper, he had worried that some vultures would take him for, not roadkill, but camper-roof kill. But that had never happened ....

Joe was indeed roused a little early—6:55 by his watch.

He pushed himself upright (he was still on top of the sleeping bag because the night had been warm), and climbed down the ladder, grabbing the bag on the way. He and the builders greeted each other.

Joe pointed to the envelope.

"May rain today, but we should have it in dry by noon," the husband said.

Joe nodded and went to his pickup as several trucks with workmen pulled up. Joe waved to them and left for his workplace.

Joe met with a few clients that morning. As he was checking his e-mail, one of the technicians came in to tell him the two repairmen were there and working on the two instruments that were down. Joe went to talk to them, just touching base. One of the instruments needed a part, but miraculously the guy had it in his van. Joe needed authorization to buy the part, so he went to see Hope Dearing.

Her door was closed. Joe knocked.

There were some sounds Joe couldn't interpret, and then a muffled voice said, "Come in."

Joe handed the authorization form to Hope for her signature. She scribbled something on the paper and handed it back to Joe without looking at him. Even so, Joe could tell she had been crying: her mascara was smudged, her eyes were red, and she seemed utterly forlorn. Joe was tempted to offer comfort, a response honed by years of meeting with upset people, but he realized that would be inappropriate, so he just took the signed authorization form away, closing the door quietly behind him.

Once the two instruments were back online, Joe heated something in the microwave, ate it, and met with more clients. Then he prepared some reports for the mail. He heard a rumble. Looking out, he could see storm clouds gathering. He checked his watch: just after four. He hoped the rafters were up and the plywood was nailed on them. He would see soon.

He had an e-mail from the journal. It was a little soon, he thought. Joe hoped this didn't mean the paper had been turned down, but he had to open the file. For a while, he stared at the letter without understanding it. Finally he realized that it had been accepted, but some changes were necessary. He read them. There weren't very many, and he gradually understood they weren't major. He had them done in fifteen minutes.

It all seemed too easy. Joe reread everything more carefully, and checked the revisions and changes. It was done! He sent the revised manuscript back, plus copies to his adviser and coauthor at the university. After a long minute, the computer told Joe the e-mails had gone through. Joe couldn't believe it. He sighed, stretched, and tried to feel happy. But that would take a while.

Joe checked on the lab. Everything was operational. No clients were waiting. There were some mailings to be made, and Joe tried to settle down enough to make them. The rumblings outside became louder, more definite, a real thunderstorm. Joe forced himself to concentrate. Soon he had sent everything.

Two e-mails. One was from the journal, the other from Penny. Joe opened the one from the journal, expecting a routine acknowledgment of receipt. Instead, it said the paper was accepted and was now "in press." Joe sent a copy of the acceptance letter to his adviser, another to the coauthor who had done the carbon 14 analysis, and, after thinking about it, a copy of the revised, accepted manuscript to Penny. At this point, he remembered to check Penny's e-mail:

> Joe, you aren't going to believe this, but these people were Tocharians from Central Asia, the Tarim Basin. They spoke and wrote an Indo-European language and they were Buddhists. How and why they made it here is a real mystery.

Joe replied:

> Penny, my paper has been accepted. I just sent you a copy of the final version. Tocharians? Never heard of them, or of the Tarim Basin. I am thinking the bunch

that ended up here was running from something. The Chinese? Why did they leave?

Turkik-speaking tribes took over. About 600 CE. Many of the Tocharians stayed, but apparently some, maybe just the leaders, left. By the way, Tocharians is the name given them by the Greeks. We aren't sure what they called themselves. But they were literate, spoke and wrote a language related to ancient Iranian, Greek, Celtic, Germanic, but that wouldn't have helped them here.

So they were actually a lost tribe.

Yeah. That's the title: Lost Tribe.

Okay. Yeah, good. I heard the Paiutes claimed these people were cannibals. That doesn't sound like Buddhists.

I think that was a slur, a justification, put about by the Paiutes. To justify what they did. People think of the Native Americans as victims, which of course they often were, but they were and are human beings, and living, or trying to live, in north-central Nevada, and suddenly having this group of people appear who looked totally different, acted different, who were trying to take some of what must have been very limited food, well, you can see what must have happened.

Joe could see this. He had another question:

How did they make a living? In the Tarim Basin, I mean.

They raised cattle, horses, and sheep, and grew crops. But coming thousands of miles to Nevada, they would probably have lost any means of making a living except hunting. And that, as I said, made them direct competitors of the Paiutes.

No horses?

No. All the horses in the Americas were brought here by the Spanish. The Native Americans apparently hunted the horses originally here to extinction.

Damn. You've done your homework, Penny.

Joe, your paper has just arrived. That is great. My boss is going to be very happy. Now what about the newspaper article?

Penny, I want you to write the article, since you know who these people were. You're first author. Just get my name right: Joseph P. Stallings.

What does the P stand for?

Patrick. What is your middle name?

Marie.

So the authors will be Penny M. Echeverria and Joseph P. Stallings. Your fame is assured. Say, is the Tarim Basin desert or what?

It is a lot like the area near Lovelock, I think.

But there was a tribe living there already.

And that would have been the cause of the antagonism.

Let me know what I can contribute, technical and otherwise.

Right. I will get on this. How is your house coming along?

The builders thought they could get the roof on today—and none too soon because there is a thunderstorm going on.

Joe, we will need to get together to get this article in finished form.

This Sunday is fine. My place or yours?

My parents' place has a roof, so it had better be my place.

The sparkling wine okay?

Yes! See you Sunday at two.

Joe looked outside. The rain was easing already, and it was time to leave. Joe took his usual look outside and went through the labs and office. All clear. He went to the Pizza Hut, got a Supreme and a big drink, and drove to his place, which was now taking shape.

The builders had been right about what they would get done today. The plywood was on, and even the tarpaper. Despite the storm, everything looked intact. The air was moist; it smelled good. There were a few small puddles in the creek, shrinking rapidly because the ground had been dry. Joe sat on the steps of his camper and ate his pizza and drank his Pepsi. He now felt very much at peace. Soon he would have a real house, a real home, a place he could bring a wife—no, a place he could bring Penny.

Joe reproached himself almost at once. She might have someone .... but somehow Joe didn't think so. Well, the article would bring them together enough for him to see if anything more would come of it. But he hoped, he hoped so much, she could come share his life. He was so very lonely.

PARANOIA'S REWARD

Saturday was business as usual—usual for Saturdays, that is. There were many customers, often requiring sympathetic handling. This was emotionally wearing as well as time consuming. There were problems with the equipment, mostly minor but all demanding attention. It went without saying that Hope Dearing was no help, but at least she was staying out of the way. She had moved from appearing emotionally stricken to just looking depressed. Joe would have sympathized, but his sympathy supply was all being consumed professionally.

Still, Joe was feeling upbeat. Tomorrow he would drive to Winnemucca to meet Penny's parents. She had sent the directions to the Echeverria's sheep ranch, repeating her request that he arrive at 2:00 p.m. She had also sent a first draft of the article, and Joe had again talked to the editor, who was sounding more interested.

The roof of Joe's house had been shingled, and many of the interior walls were in, the plumbing was nearly finished, and the wiring had been run into place. Once the flooring was laid, the appliances would be installed, including a big hot water heater, enough capacity for two bathrooms and the dishwasher.

Even so, by evening Joe was more than ready to head home—
it was nearing that status. Out of habit, Joe, after turning out the
lights, looked outside carefully for anyone lurking or loitering
near the GeneQuestion building. And this evening there was
someone: a man staying in the shadows but near enough to the
door to catch Joe when he came out. Joe couldn't think of anyone
doing such a thing unless he intended to harm Joe. Joe took out
his cell phone, dialed 911, and spoke to the dispatcher.

She asked, "Is he armed?"

Joe thought, and then said, "I don't know. I just don't want to
find out the hard way that he is."

"Stay inside until the police get there. They are on their way."

"Right."

Within a matter of seconds, two police cars had appeared,
and four cops came out, guns drawn, yelling, "Stop."

Joe opened the door and saw the police officers run into the
bushes the man had been skulking in.

Joe stood there at the door to his workplace. Another cop
car appeared. A detective got out and came over. Joe pointed to
where the others had gone. The detective spoke into a mike on
his shoulder, and then Joe heard someone say, "We got him."

Several minutes passed. Finally, two of the cops appeared,
holding a man while two more officers followed. One was
carrying a plastic bag with a gun in it. The skulk, who was
handcuffed, was put into one of the police cars, which was then
driven away, lights flashing. The two other cops came over. Both
were breathing heavily.

The detective asked Joe, "Can you come to the station to ID
this guy?"

"I didn't see his face, just his shadow. All I can say is I think
it was a guy."

"Just to see if you know him."

"Sure. Let me get my truck, and I'll drive there right away."

The detective nodded, and Joe, who was getting a little shaky,
went to find his truck.

Joe managed to get to the police station without hitting anyone or anything and went inside. Another detective let Joe look through a one-way glass at the man, who was sitting at a table, still handcuffed. The man was demanding to talk to a lawyer. Joe got the impression the man had been through all this before. He was dark and bulky but otherwise unremarkable and unfamiliar.

Joe looked at the detective and shrugged. "Let me know what you find when you ID this guy, will you?"

The detective took Joe's cell phone number, and Joe headed home. He didn't feel hungry.

Joe spent the night in the house, lying on the sleeping bag on the floor. There was a threat of rain again, and he didn't want to be cooped up inside the camper. He got up a little late Sunday morning and drove to McDonald's for breakfast. He used the restroom there, ate, and then went to a liquor store. The sparkling wine was still in stock, and Joe bought a bottle. He then went to the office, showered, shaved, and put on fresh clothes. By now it was nearly noon.

Joe was in his truck when his cell phone went off. He answered. The voice on the other end identified himself as Detective Ferguson, and Joe remembered the name from the previous night.

"We ID'd the guy. He has a big rap sheet, mostly armed robbery, some assaults. He has a warrant out on him from LA, and we're going to extradite him there because here we can only nail him for being a convicted felon with a gun. Otherwise he isn't talking."

"Thank you for the info. At least he'll be off the street for a while."

"Do you think your ex is involved?"

Joe had told the cops about his suspicions and said, "That's my guess. But I can't be sure."

"Okay then."

"Thanks for telling me."

Joe headed east on I-80. He would get there about two o'clock, as Penny had requested. She had also asked Joe to park behind the barn, which seemed odd. And why wasn't she asking him to lunch? Well, he would find out soon.

The Echeverrias lived about twenty miles from Winnemucca. At the western Winnemucca exit, Joe turned north on US Highway 95. He drove through the town, which didn't take long, and crossed the railroad tracks—the old UP-CP, the first transcontinental rail line anywhere. About ten miles farther north, Joe turned right, to follow a dusty gravel road. The Little Humboldt River ran to his left. It sparkled in the sun. The country to either side wasn't barren, but there certainly wasn't much vegetation, though evidently there was enough for sheep.

Joe got to the wood-framed, two-story house, which had a couple of trees near where rain from the gutters was directed. The paint, originally white, was peeling. But after Joe got out, there was Penny to welcome him. They both broke into grins. Joe got the bottle of sparkling wine and showed it to Penny to her clear approval, and the two of them went inside.

Two older people stood inside, obviously Penny's parents. Penny introduced him. "This is Dr. Joe Stallings, ideally my coauthor on the newspaper article we're writing together."

Joe shook hands with both of them. They seemed friendly enough, a little reserved—no, Joe decided, a little sad. Odd again. They were in a big room, evidently a dining room, with long tables and benches, like picnic tables. Otherwise, the room was empty.

"Come this way," said Penny, and she led Joe to an office. There was a desk and chair as well as a table with two more chairs. The table held a plate with two loose-meat subs and glasses on coasters. This time Joe had come prepared. He pulled a folding corkscrew out of his pocket, brandished it, and opened the wine bottle. Penny was amused. Joe poured two glasses, and he and Penny sat down to eat, sipping at the wine.

In truth, Joe was thirsty enough to drink the whole bottle,

but he remembered his manners and the fact that he would have to drive back when they had finished. They sat down together in front of Penny's PC; she called up the article and scrolled slowly through it while Joe read.

Penny had done a good job. She had even scaled the length of the article to what usually was printed in a Sunday supplement. She had also dug up cuttings from newspaper accounts of the time and a photograph comparing the skeleton of the man whose molars had yielded so much information and a presumably normal-sized man. The face Joe had reconstructed was at the end, staring hauntingly at the reader.

Joe made some minor changes, saw a few typos and one error: "Penny," he said, "it's lactase persistence, not lactose persistence. Change the o to an a."

Penny did so and then asked, "What's the difference?"

Joe, happy to show off his knowledge, told her, "Spelled with an a, it's an enzyme; with an o, it's a sugar. Most Native Americans lose their ability to digest the sugar after they are weaned. They lose the enzyme. Europeans and people of European origin are still able to drink milk as adults because they still have the enzyme."

"Oh."

"This is good. Send it to my computer, and I'll send it to the editor—whether she wants it or not."

Penny smiled and forwarded the article as an e-mail attachment, a big one with all the figures. Joe poured two more glasses.

He raised his: "To fame." They both drank, and then Joe added, "Though I hear fortune is better."

Penny laughed and asked Joe, "Why is your place on something called Gold Creek? Was it worked out?"

Joe looked around, leaned toward Penny, and told her, "Don't tell anyone else about this." Penny nodded, and Joe resumed, "The creek is usually dry, but I did some panning when it had water in it and cleared more than a hundred thousand dollars' worth of gold. I'm paying for the house with it. Whether there is any more, I just don't know. I hope there is."

Penny, smiling, shook her head. She was clearly very impressed, and Joe was expecting to be invited to stay for dinner. However, she turned serious and said, "Joe, I would really like to ask you to stay for dinner, but I can't. There are reasons—some things I don't want to talk about."

Joe of course replied, "It's okay, Penny. Enjoy the rest of the champagne. But not too much, 'cause you have to go to work tomorrow."

Penny smiled once more and got up. So did Joe, and they went out together, through the back door and out behind the barn where Joe's truck was parked—no, he thought suddenly, concealed from anyone driving by. Joe and Penny stopped at the truck. Penny extended her hand, and Joe took it. It wasn't a handshake but something very different. Penny's hand was soft.

Joe and Penny looked into each other's eyes. Penny could probably see the loneliness in Joe's, but Joe could certainly see the sadness in Penny's. He raised her hand and kissed it. Penny looked around and then leaned forward. Joe did the same. They kissed. Penny's lips were so soft, thought Joe. But he restrained himself from kissing her again, though he really wanted to. He just said, "I'll let you know the score as soon as I find out what it is."

Penny nodded. Joe released her hand and turned to his truck, unlocked the door, and got into it. He attached the seat belt, started the engine, and waved to Penny, who waved back. Joe left for his home.

On I-80, Joe noted his gas tank was getting a little low and pulled off to gas up again at a station near Lovelock. He was trying to figure out what was bothering Penny and, yes, Penny's folks. A rival? One of the shepherds nearby? A jealous rival? Someone her folks wanted her to marry? Some cousin who would inherit their place? It sounded mid-Victorian, but maybe Penny's folks still thought that way. There was no sign of a brother or sister.

Joe shook his head. When his gas tank was full, he collected his credit card receipt and went on his way.

Back in Carson City, Joe decided to kill a little time by looking at the furniture in Goodwill. He saw several pieces: a desk and chair, a big leather couch, a bed, and a dresser. The prices were okay, but Joe was getting hungry and stopped at Pizza Hut for his usual. He thought he could move the furniture himself, once the house was finished.

Joe decided to eat in his own place, even standing up at the counter. A look around depressed him even more: dust, bits of wood, but mostly empty, empty space. Joe tried to imagine what life would be like if Penny lived here as well. Children? If possible: Joe guessed both he and Penny were getting on. Furniture would help, but mostly the place needed someone— her—to fill the emptiness, not just in the house but in Joe's life, in Joe's soul.

Joe washed the last of the pizza down with the last of his Pepsi and then walked out the back door to check the generator. There was still plenty of gas; everything was humming. Joe went to his camper, got his sleeping bag and carried it up to the empty, dusty, so-called "master bedroom." Then he went down to the kitchen sink, opened the faucet, and filled the cup the Pepsi had come in with his own water from his own well. The hot water heater was on order, so temporary connections gave cold water only. It tasted just fine. Joe emptied his bladder in his own toilet and flushed it. He was home—an empty home for now, but home.

KEEPING IN TOUCH

Joe woke up when the builders and the workmen came in. He looked at his alarm clock: just short of seven. He got up, folded his sleeping bag, and went downstairs. His appearance surprised everyone; the builders thought he was in the camper. The male builder asked Joe for the last $20,000. Joe wrote out the check and handed it to him.

"We'll clean this place up," the builder said, gesturing toward the floor, "and then move the appliances in." Nodding at Estelle, he added, "We wondered if you would sell us the camper, unless you plan to use it yourself."

Joe nodded, gave the builders the price he had paid for the camper, and added, "If that's okay, I'll move my stuff out this evening."

The man nodded and told Joe, "There will be about thirteen hundred dollars left to pay, so we'll subtract the amount you quoted from that."

"Fine," Joe said and walked out to his truck.

On the way to work, Joe wondered if he should have asked for more. Then he decided he'd been fair, and that was okay. Once cleaned up, Joe had to deal with the usual issues and did so. Finally, there was a break in the action and he could call the editor of the local paper he had talked to before.

He told her, "I can send you the e-mail of the article I've talked to you about. I think it is well researched, well written by my coauthor, and of more than local interest."

The woman gave Joe an e-mail address to use, and Joe sent the article.

About midafternoon, Joe got a call from the police.

"That guy who was hanging around your place has been extradited back to LA" the officer said.

"Did he ever say why he was hanging around here?"

"No, he wouldn't talk." There was a moment of silence, and then the detective went on, "Just one thing: the guy was living in Lost Wages. What he was doing up here, we don't know."

For an instant, Joe wondered once again if Stacey, his ex-wife, had sent someone to attack him. But he had told the police about his suspicions, and they hadn't been able to locate Stacey, at least under her maiden name.

"Thanks for the info."

"Right," said the cop.

As Joe went to meet with more soon-to-be-very-unhappy clients, he tried to shake off the feeling that there was more going on with the poles of his life, his ex, his job, Penny, than he really knew. But he still had to earn his living, and through the rest of the day, he did his best. At last Joe was able to sit down, have a Pepsi, and check his e-mail. The Sunday supplement editor told Joe the article would be published two weeks from the previous day. Joe forwarded the note to Penny, remembered he had to clean out his camper, and carefully checked out the neighborhood before leaving.

Both floors of Joe's home had been vacuumed. The appliances were in. Joe checked the refrigerator. It was cold, so he filled the ice cube trays and set them inside the freezer compartment. No automatic ice maker here—not that Joe minded. He went to the camper and began shifting boxes piled with books (those that had survived his ex's temper tantrums), and set the boxes on the bookshelves. He transferred his clothes and even began hanging them up in his bedroom. Then he moved his sleeping bag, went back for a final sweep of the camper, and came back inside. Now Joe was home. All he needed was furniture, and he would get that this coming Sunday.

The alarm clock woke Joe rather than trucks or pickups full of workers. No painting had been done in his place because Joe wanted Penny to choose the colors—that is, if he could persuade her to join him .... Joe was able to clean up, shave, and leave for work like a human being should be able to do, as opposed to a homeless man, for the first time in years. As he drove to work, though, all he could think about, aside from Penny, was that he had to get things at Walmart: soap, laundry detergent, shower curtains for the two tubs .... He had better make a list when he had time. First and foremost, he would see if that couch was still available at Goodwill. Joe was damned if he was going to sleep on the floor again.

This day was slower, mercifully, and Joe had started his list when he received an e-mail from corporate HQ. It asked Joe what all the technicians and other people in the Carson City branch thought about Joe's boss, Hope Dearing. He was also asked to keep it quiet. Joe knew what the rest of the people in the lab and office thought about Hope, and it wasn't likely to win her any pay raises. Perhaps it was because of Joe's well-honed sympathy toward anyone who was unhappy, but he didn't want to hurt her further. The two of them had reached a good working relationship, and Joe didn't want to disturb this. And he didn't like the idea of sneaking around behind her back, digging up dirt. So after thinking some more, he wrote out a carefully phrased reply in longhand, corrected it, and then typed it:

> All I know is that Dr. Dearing and I have put together
> a very profitable, efficient, and harmonious operation.
> She is in charge and should get the credit.
>
> J. Stallings

Joe thought of showing Dearing the e-mail and his reply, but she still seemed unhappy. Instead he went on his lab rounds, checking the performances of the instruments, the inventory, talking to the techs, and trying to head off any problems before they led to shutdowns. All was well for now; tomorrow might be .... Well, tomorrow would be its own problem.

That evening, Joe got the couch—shiny leather, with two shiny leather cushions—a desk and a chair, and managed to get them all in the back of his pickup. He drove home carefully, turned his truck so its rear was nearly touching the front steps, and managed to pull, wrestle, and drag the couch just inside the house. He eventually turned it on one end, tipped it over, and turned it on its other end, until it was where he wanted it. He left it facing the Franklin stove. The cushions and chair were next, and easy. Next was the desk. Joe was barely able to get the thing into the living room, turning it and tipping it the way he had moved the couch. Then he gave up. He would finish the job tomorrow. As before, Joe ate dinner standing up—or rather, slumped. He decided some more chairs would be next. Then he went to bed on the couch.

Joe hadn't turned the air-conditioning on yet, since the house was empty most of the time. Still, the air inside was not too hot when he came home. He had left the doors to the balconies open, though not the screen doors. When he had opened the front door, he could feel the draft. He left the screen doors closed. Still, the gentle movement of cooler night air let Joe sleep.

Despite his worries about sliding off the slick surface, Joe slept soundly—so soundly that the alarm clock had nearly run down before he finally got up the next morning. After bathroom duties, Joe decided that some groceries, especially Pepsi, and then some chairs—no, bar stools—would be next on his list. He edged around the desk, lying reproachfully on its side, nearly blocking the door.

"This evening, for sure," Joe told the desk, and stepped out into bright sunshine. He got in his truck and drove to work.

It was average day, but Joe was feeling stiff from loading and moving furniture the previous day.

There was an e-mail from Penny:

>Joe, is your house finished?

Joe replied:

>It doesn't have much furniture yet, but I'm working on that. It is starting to feel like a real home, my first, I mean, of my own.

>What are your folks doing?

>My dad kept the books for a Ford dealership in Reno. But he and my mom are now back in Michigan, living near Detroit, retired.

>Do you have any brothers or sisters?

>One sister, twelve years older. She has an MD, and a private practice near Lansing. She also has two kids.

>Married?

>Yes. She and her husband have a joint practice. Do you have any brothers or sisters?

>No. Something about a Jesus factor.

>Rhesus factor.

>I guess. Anyway, my cousin will inherit the ranch, so an Echeverria will carry on the line.

>You okay with that?

>Yes. I wasn't sure what I wanted to do, just go to college. I was a history major, like I told you. Then I got married after my third year, so that dream went out the window.

What were you going to do with the history degree?

Teach school, I guess. I wasn't thinking of going any further—well, maybe an MA.

You could finish up, get your degree online.

I've been looking into that. I plan to start this fall.

Good.

You approve?

If it keeps you off the streets and out of the bars, it's a clear gain for community standards of, well, I don't want to get too explicit.

Joe, you are bad. I'll sign off now. I suppose you need to shop.

I do, and will. Sweet dreams, my princess, happy visions, and may tomorrow's and every day's realities transcend them all.

Joe got some groceries. He checked his watch and decided to swing by Goodwill and see if they were open and had what he wanted. They were and did. He bought a set of six bar chairs, not stools: they had backs and even armrests. He took them to his place, backed his truck up to the stairs as before, and unloaded everything. Joe was thinking in terms of a party, with the Hershes, another couple from Joe's defense, and of course Penny. Then he remembered his promise to the desk. He decided a token effort would have to do, and once more lifted it by one end and then tipped it enough to shift it without scraping the floor or the desk. Once he'd started, he kept on, finally setting one end down in the room with the bookshelves. He would set it upright tomorrow. Now sweating, tired, and sore, he would sleep well.

Next morning saw a further advance toward a civilized life: Joe microwaved a breakfast burrito, washed it down with a cold Pepsi, brushed his teeth, and drove to work. Although he was later than usual, he could start work right away. Just as well: for some unknown reason, clients with unsolvable problems, some major meltdowns of equipment, complex procurement issues, all part of the day—in fact each issue enough to occupy an entire day—occurred at once. Joe tried to prioritize, but found he was falling further behind in every direction. No lunch. Joe had to stay past five, past six talking to clients. It was a quarter past seven before he could leave.

Joe bought a dresser from Goodwill and a number one combo from Burger King and got back near sundown. The dresser wasn't too heavy, but it was awkward. He was able to get it inside the house, but that was all. He sat down in one of his chairs at the kitchen counter, ate and drank, used the toilet, then set the desk upright. He pushed the chair under the desk and thought he had done his limit. He fell asleep, wondering how he was going to get the dresser upstairs.

Getting ready for work seemed slow and awkward. Joe was finally ready to leave when he realized he could take the drawers out of the dresser, move them, and then move the dresser much more easily. At work, he managed to catch up with the clients, got Hope Dearing to approve the repairs and orders, and dealt with some personnel issue involving vacations and parking. It wasn't as bad as it had been the day before, but he was very glad to hang it up at six.

He was just leaving when he saw an e-mail from Penny:

> Joe, thank you for the farewell. I've been called a few things but "princess" isn't one of them. I was just, well, a little overcome.

Joe replied:

> My usual effect, at least on princesses.

It kind of made up for the crack about public health and safety.

I didn't say anything about public health and safety. Please don't overinterpret.

Okay, but leaving things to my imagination is a little risky.

I'll keep that in mind.

Any more furniture?

Buying the stuff isn't so bad; it's hauling it into the house and setting it in its place. And that's just on the first floor.

Can't you get any help?

No. I never made many friends growing up.

Why not?

I suppose it's because I was kind of an afterthought, a surprise, to my parents. My sister had no time for me, I was so much younger, and my parents were focused on her. So I grew up alone, shy, awkward. It didn't help that my parents figured that since they were so old when I was conceived and born, I must be suffering from some genetic defect or other.

Are you?

No, but that is probably why I decided to go into genetics, if only to understand what they were talking about.

But you have done all right, after all.

Yeah, except for the shy, awkward part. I guess I will never really get over that, though having to deal with clients who are upset over the results has probably helped.

I see. Are you effectively in charge of your operation? Do you have deputies or assistants?

I have to deal with everything. I have a boss, but I am a general and universal factotum.

Maybe you will get promoted.

There have been a couple of odd e-mails from the management, asking about my boss: what I think of her, what the other people think of her.

What did you say?

My boss and I have a good relationship, and I don't want to have to break in a new boss. I told them that we were doing a good job here and she should get the credit.

Maybe you will get the job.

I'm not sure I would like that. She seems kind of sad lately, and I don't want to hurt her any more.

I will sign off now. Careful with that furniture. You need to stay healthy.

I'll keep that in mind too. Sleep, my princess.

This evening, Joe went to Lowes. He decided to spring for some new stuff. He wound up getting shower curtains for both bathrooms, some curtains and curtain rods, and a couple of deck chairs for the balconies. He also got some carryout Chinese, since he now had a fridge and microwave, and drove back, checking, as he always did, for people following him.

Joe moved everything inside his place, looked at the gas level in his power generator, and then sat down to a real meal. As was usual with Chinese, he had about four times what he could reasonably eat, but he did his best, eating about one and a half times what he usually did. He was able to carry the deck chairs up and set them on the two balconies. He wondered if setting both side by side in one might be better .... Maybe lying next to Penny, looking together toward either Carson City or the dark, silent mountains to the southeast .... He shook off the thought and managed to haul the emptied dresser up the stairs and into his bedroom. That done, Joe decided it was time to sleep, so once more he bedded down on the couch after setting the alarm.

And once more he woke up stiff as hell. He figured all the exercise he was getting must be making him stronger, but it was a slow process. A good hot shower might have helped, but not a lot. Joe got to work in time and started with the day's clients, dealt with repairs, purchases, saw an equipment saleswoman and promised to consider buying her company's product, saw more clients, mailed reports of results to other clients, snatched ten minutes to eat something microwaved, and so on through the day. By the time Joe could leave, it was nearly dark. He realized he hadn't seen Dearing that day and found himself wondering if she was all right. There were no more e-mails and no skulks, and Joe went to buy groceries.

Joe had more of the Chinese and then decided to take his sleeping bag and set it on one of the deck chairs, as it was a fine night.

Unfortunately, Joe wasn't used to sleeping on a deck chair, so he went inside and finished the night on the couch. That night, he had nightmares: he was being bullied, he couldn't defend himself, and he was going to be humiliated in front of Penny .... Joe woke, shaking and sweating, and got up a few minutes early.

It was a reasonably easy day. Dearing was in, but Joe could see she had been crying again, so he bothered her as little as possible and made sure no one else bothered her. Another e-mail from HQ announced that a couple of big shots were coming to "inspect operations." ETA: two days. Joe didn't like this at all. He figured she was going to be fired and either he'd be put in her place or someone else would. Joe decided he would walk Dearing through the finances and then brief her on new equipment available and what he thought they should get. After this he would walk her around the lab, effectively introducing her to everyone, trying to get them all to play nice when the big shots called.

Joe went to see her, taking a brief summary of the finances. She hadn't read the e-mail, and he warned her that this visit was likely to have unpleasant consequences for one of them, and began the briefing.

She listened quietly, and then asked Joe, "Does everyone want to get rid of me?"

"I don't, and have said so. We're a good team, and breaking up a good team is stupid."

Joe finished his briefing, made sure she could remember the details, and told her about the proposed new piece of equipment. He explained its advantages, which were basically that it would do the slowest step in their operations much faster and increase output. Joe showed her the figures and gave her the piece of paper they were written on, along with the projected return. Then he persuaded her to go into the lab, where they discussed where the new piece of equipment would go. He brought three of the technicians into the discussion, making sure everyone understood that Dearing was the moving force behind it all. Joe saw her glance at him, a glance he couldn't interpret, but she went along. They toured the rest of the place, Joe unobtrusively making sure everyone got the impression that she was just checking on everything and Joe was her faithful assistant. Then she went to lunch and Joe heated something—it looked great on the label, at least.

That evening, Joe bought a bed for himself, the first real bed he had had in years. He also bought several discounted rugs. Back at his place, he exhausted himself hauling most of them up the stairs. The mattress and springs were the worst. Once they were moved, Joe microwaved a Mexican dinner and ate, washing it down with Pepsi over ice cubes. Joe felt better, but not better enough to unroll the rugs and assemble the bed. As he fell asleep on the couch, Joe decided, reluctantly, that he would have to get two more beds and dressers for the two empty bedrooms, but he wasn't going to rush that.

The next day was the visit: two suits, trying to be reassuring. Over the years of having to deal with customers who were often upset, Joe had developed a sense of what was in their minds. The two men were about Joe's height and build, dressed almost identically except for their ties. This was a little overdressed for Nevada, and their attempts to put Joe at ease made him more uneasy. There weren't any clients to meet until the afternoon, so Joe took the visitors into the room where he met clients. He offered them Pepsis, but they said no thanks. Joe sat back and sipped his Pepsi while the suit complimented Joe on the success of his branch.

Joe told them his boss deserved the credit: "We all work for her. She's in charge."

The suits nodded and then questioned Joe about his qualifications. Joe answered, taking care to give credit for his PhD to the liberal policies of the company. The suits glanced at each other and then got down to cases:

"Joe," one said, "who meets with clients?"

"Me."

"Not Dr. Dearing?"

"I've been doing it for a long time now, and Dr. Dearing didn't want to make changes in a system that works."

"Who does routine ordering and deals with maintenance issues?"

"Me, after clearing them with Dr. Dearing. We're going to order an upgraded instrument that will increase output and, we figure, pay for itself within three years. Dr. Dearing has the figures. The company gives us flexibility in doing things like that, which one of the reasons we all like to work here."

The two suits nodded and then one said, "We'll speak to Dr. Dearing."

As they rose to leave, one of them asked Joe, "Is there a publication coming out?"

"Yes. It's been accepted for publication and mentions the company. As a matter of fact, there will be an article in the local Sunday supplement next week that puts the dissertation findings in context. My affiliation here is mentioned, of course."

Both men seemed impressed but left after shaking Joe's hand. Joe shrugged and prayed that Hope Dearing would survive. He couldn't really figure why the two had come. He hoped he had put out whatever fire had brought them.

Joe didn't see the two suits again. He was fully occupied with clients and routine matters until after everyone else had left. At this point he checked outside and left himself. He hadn't seen anything of Hope. He went straight to his place while keeping an eye out for anyone following him. No one was, and Joe ate leftovers, then unrolled carpets, assembled the bed and dresser. He briefly thought of sleeping on the bed, but had no sheets, pillows, or blankets. That's next, thought Joe as he went downstairs to the sofa again.

Joe didn't see the suits or, for that matter, Hope the next day. Otherwise it was just another day. Nothing from Penny. Since Joe was able to leave a little earlier, he could do more shopping. He got another bed and dresser, both smaller than the one in his room, some sheets and blankets, and more towels for the bathrooms. He also got stuff from the grocery, as well as laundry detergent to wash the sheets and towels. He took everything back home and, having done the preliminaries for the washing, as it were, just ate and went to sleep, his conscience eased.

HOPE

The next day was well along when Joe got an order form for reagents. The lab bought them ready-made because preparing them from scratch was too time-consuming. And Joe didn't trust the water they could get, never mind having the deionizer and accessories needed to maintain it as well. Joe took the form to Hope's office and knocked on the door.

He hadn't seen her yet today, but he heard a muffled voice say, "Yes? What is it, Joe?"

Joe was the only person from the lab who ever talked to her, and he figured she probably recognized his knock. When he went in, Hope looked up from her desk, where she had been sitting with her head in her arms, crying. Joe had never seen anyone look so wretched, so defeated. His impulse was to take her in his arms and try to comfort her, but he knew that was completely unprofessional.

He closed the door, sat down, and said in his quietest, gentlest voice, "Do you want to talk about it?"

"Joe, I just got word I am out, fired. You are going to be my replacement. I'm sure you will do a better job than I did."

Joe shook his head, but Hope went on, "Joe, I did something

98

I shouldn't have. I listened to your meeting with those two from the company headquarters. I was afraid you would try to get me out, but instead you were completely loyal. I was a little ashamed of myself, but I was also proud of you. You are a good, decent man, and one of my biggest regrets is that we won't be seeing each other again, just when I was beginning to appreciate you."

Here Hope stopped to blow her nose and wipe her eyes. Joe remembered that the conference room was bugged (in case any of the clients became suicidal or homicidal), and remained silent.

"I had a boyfriend," Hope said. "I was expecting him to marry me, but he kept putting things off. I was supporting him because he had lost his job. On top of losing mine—I told him about it— he went and cleaned out my bank account, my rent is overdue, and the landlord told me to leave. Everything I own is in my car, and I'll probably have to sleep in it. I have nothing, no future that I can see. I can't even afford gas to drive back east to where I grew up. I just came in to clean out my desk."

Joe sat back, stunned. "No one has said anything to me about your replacement," he said. "Look, my place is short of furniture, but I can buy more. Someone should stay there—I mean, when I'm here. You can stay as long as you like, or if you want to drive back east, I'll give you money. But staying at my place will allow you to rest and recover. It's a nice place, really, it is."

"Where is your place?"

"Southeast of Carson City. On a dry creek called Gold Creek."

Joe remembered his order form.

"I've got to get this stuff ordered. Let me check my e-mail. If I'm your replacement, I'll order these things myself. Put your stuff in your car. It's a slow day right now. I'll lead you to my place, and you can decide."

Joe got up, and Hope's face brightened a little. Joe nodded to her, went to his office, and turned on his computer. Sure enough, there was a message from HQ:

To Joseph P. Stallings, PhD:

Effective receipt of this e-mail, you are promoted to
head of the Carson City/Reno section. Congratulations.

And Joe was expected to click on the Received icon. After a moment, he did so because he had to get those reagents ordered. After another moment, he printed out the message in case there were questions. He took the printout and the order to the woman who did procurement, initialed the order, and showed her the message.

She was delighted, telling several people within earshot, "Hey, Hopeless was fired and Joe is the new head."

This made Joe wince, and he thought the joy everyone expressed was excessive. "Okay, no more Mr. Nice Guy," he growled.

This convulsed everyone, making even Joe smile, but he left as soon as he could. He went back to Hope's—now his—office, knocked, heard her say, "Come in," and did so.

She had everything packed in cardboard boxes, five in all, and she and Joe each picked one up. They went out to Hope's car, a black Chevy that was several years old, and set the boxes in the back. When it was full, Hope and Joe made two more trips and set the rest of the boxes in the passenger's side. Joe described his pickup and went to get it. He pulled up next to Hope's car and she started it. Then she followed Joe out to his place.

Hope was very impressed with Joe's house. Joe unlocked the door, and they began shifting her things inside. He showed her the other bedroom with a bed and dresser.

He told her, "I haven't washed the new sheets or blankets or towels yet."

"I'll deal with them."

Joe was very glad to hear it, and showed her where the new things were piled on the washing machine.

"Where do you sleep?" Hope asked.

Joe pointed to the couch. Hope shook her head, and Joe gave

her his cell phone number. "Think of what you want for dinner and let me know," he said.

She nodded, and Joe went back to work.

Joe decided to stay in his old office, at least for now. He told himself everyone knew where to find him. Remarkably, he didn't have to meet with any clients that day, but a large number had to get their results by mail. When he was finished with that, Joe emerged to check on the staff. There was a holiday mood that made Joe cringe, but he tried not to show it. Just Mr. Stone Face. No party, no early leave, there's work to do. That got people focused again.

One of the office staff asked if Joe was going to move into Dearing's office. She added that she and her two colleagues needed more room.

Joe blinked at this and then decided. "All right. I'll stay where I am, and you three can move to Dr. Dearing's office. You'll need to rearrange things."

Their desks were smaller than Dearing's, but there was plenty of space in her office. The three staffers looked very pleased. Joe arranged for the janitor to help with the move.

So far, so good, but that left the assignment of the director's parking space open. Several people voiced an interest in it, since everyone knew Joe parked someplace else. Joe didn't know what to do about the space. Anyone he gave it to would be his friend for life, but the people who wanted it and didn't get it would spend their spare time sticking pins into dolls intended to represent Joe. So Joe dithered. Finally he decided, and told everyone that the next director would expect that space to be open. No one was happy, but at least it was a shared unhappiness, with no winner and consequently no losers. And the space stayed open.

About six, Joe got a call from Hope.

"Joe, when will you be back?"

"In less than an hour, depending on what you want me to get."

"Maybe a pizza."

"I usually get a Supreme, thin crust."

"What's a Supreme? The thin crust is all right."

Joe said expansively, "Prepare yourself for a gourmet experience."

"If you say so."

"What about drinks?"

"Pepsi is okay."

"I'll call in the order and be on my way."

Since there were two people, Joe ordered an extra-large. He didn't have to wait more than five minutes, and got home at a quarter to seven. He and Hope sat down to eat right away. Hope was hungry. Joe guessed she hadn't eaten anything, and in fact the two of them finished the pizza.

"I washed the sheets, pillowcases, and blankets," she said. "The blankets need more drying. Otherwise I made the beds."

Joe nodded his thanks.

"Why is the creek called Gold Creek? There isn't any water in it."

Joe sat, thinking. Then he had an idea about how to keep Hope from brooding about her worthless boyfriend and lost job and maybe make more money for her and Joe.

"There is sometimes. But what I am going to tell you has to be kept quiet, absolutely quiet, No one else is to know. Okay?"

Hope's eyes became slits as she pursed her lips. However, she said, "I'll keep everything you tell me quiet, I promise."

Joe leaned forward, as if to emphasize the secrecy of what he was going to tell her, even though there was no one else within miles of where they sat.

"I paid for this house with gold panned from the creek. I don't know if there is much more. But I'll make a deal with you: if you want to pan gold from shovelfuls of dirt from the creek bed, I'll lend you my pan and shovel, and you can get water from the faucet outside. Whatever you get, we'll split it fifty-fifty. What do you say?"

Hope sat, her head resting on one hand, looking at Joe. Then she began to nod. "Okay, Joe, but you'll have to show me how. I've never panned for gold."

Joe nodded in turn. He leaned back, drank more Pepsi, and then stood up.

"It's very tedious, but if there's gold showing up in the pan, you forget that part. Let's go outside."

They went out to Joe's truck. Joe lifted the shovel out of the bed and took the pan out of the cab. It was still twilight, and there was a bright, three-quarter moon, so they could see. Joe led the way down to the creek bed. He showed Hope where he had been digging.

"The gold I got came from someplace upstream, but I haven't found where that is yet. You want spots in the bed where there are obstructions, rocks that slow the flow so the gold and sediment fall. That is what you dig up. You put the stuff in the pan—here, let me do that."

And Joe put three shovelfuls of sediment into the pan. He gave the shovel to Hope. They both went up to the house, and Joe turned on the outdoor faucet, letting plenty of water into the pan.

"The water makes the damn thing heavy as hell. Maybe I should have put only one shovelful in."

The pan was nearly full of water. Joe turned off the faucet, squatted down, grasped the pan and its contents, and began swirling. He explained the process as Hope watched, fascinated. Joe refilled the pan with water three more times. By now the amount of sediment was much less. Even by the light of the moon, the stuff remaining in the pan seemed to glow. Joe picked some pebbles out and tossed them aside. Then he saw one pebble that looked different. He pointed to it, and Hope reached down and picked it up.

"Joe, it's really heavy—I mean, for its size."

Joe added more water, finished the swirling, and straightened up.

"Let's go inside."

Joe set the pan, now nearly dry, on the counter. He and Hope looked at the pebble, the size of a pea. It gleamed.

"That's what we're looking for," acknowledged Joe.

Hope appeared entranced. A clear case of gold fever, thought Joe. The two of them looked in the pan. Joe nodded, and looked at Hope.

"Gold dust, it's called."

"How do we get it into something? It has to be weighed, doesn't it?"

"Yeah. Let me see what I've got in the glove compartment."

Joe found the Mason jar, disposable pipettes, and scintillation vials and brought them inside. He and Hope managed to put the gold dust into a scintillation vial with more water. They let the dust settle, and pipetted off the water and any bits of sand remaining. Hope hesitated and then put the pebble in the vial.

"Look," said Joe, "if you want, you can take the nugget and have it set by a jeweler in a necklace. A keepsake."

Hope looked at Joe. Joe couldn't tell what she was thinking.

"We'll see, Joe. There should be even bigger ones. Right now, we need to get the weight."

So they dried the stuff in the vial. While the microwave was going, they sat back, drinking Pepsi.

"Maybe a few hundred bucks. "Not bad for an evening's work, but take it from me, you're going to start feeling the effects tomorrow. I speak from painful experience."

"You think the source is upstream?"

"Yeah, and not too far upstream, that's my guess. The mother lode."

"I'll pan for more, and also scout upstream."

"If there's a rock formation with veins of gold in it, I'll have to get a sledgehammer and a pick."

There was silence while Joe reflected. Then he said, "Of course, the nugget may have been rolled a long way. Otherwise you're looking for quartz, quartz veins, and pebbles and pieces."

Hope nodded. "Wherever it is, I'll find it."

Joe was pleased. At the very least, this project would keep Hope busy and, yes, hopeful, aside from bringing some extra cash into their pockets. But for now, Joe looked at his watch. "I think that's it for this evening. Tomorrow I'm going to be feeling this."

"Are you going to weigh the sample?"

"Yeah, I've got the tare weight written down—somewhere." The microwave went off.

The next day, sure enough, Joe was sore as hell: shoulders, arms, even his thighs. He dealt with clients until nearly noon, made the rounds, talking to the crew—now his crew—and then got a couple of candy bars and a Pepsi. After eating them, he saw the lab was empty, so he weighed the vial with the gold dust and the nugget. He was able to find the tare weight and was agreeably surprised to find that the previous evening's take was just over $1,000. He texted Hope, as he guessed she would be outside.

An e-mail from Penny asked him to visit with the Sunday supplement copies, same time and conditions. Joe said he would, that he had news and would bring the supplements and the bubbly as requested, although he had the feeling the bubbly would be the most welcome. Penny's reply accused Joe of making her out to be a lush.

Joe replied:

> Does that mean I can forget the sparkling stuff?
>
> Don't you dare.
>
> I thought not. See you then.

Joe had several clients, the majority with children with birth defects or rather defective genes. By now he was fairly well up on treatments and told the clients about them. Still, it was a depressing afternoon. Joe sat down at his desk and began the mailings. Then he saw an e-mail from Hope:

> Joe, I think you need to get the sledgehammer and pick. And more Pepsi. For dinner, how about Mexican? A combo plate.

He replied:

Don't know when I will be home. But will do.

As soon as he could, Joe called in his order to the Mexican restaurant he patronized. Then he went to a grocery and then to a hardware store. He got a sledgehammer, two pointed steel rods, and a metal bucket. It was still full light when he got home. He brought dinner in, saw Hope was very excited, went out and got the Pepsis, filled a pair of glasses with ice, and poured Pepsi over the cubes. Hope set out the food, plates, knives, and forks and they both sat down.

Joe was hungry. So was Hope, apparently. Finally, they were able to talk.

"Joe, I think I found the source of the gold. And I panned about ten shovelfuls."

Joe was impressed, especially when Hope brought the other scintillation vial out. It was nearly full. Joe shook his head. "That's a few thousand at least." He looked out the window. The sun was nearly down. "Let's take a look at what you found."

They went out into the fading light and walked up the creek bed to where a big ridge of rock cut across the creek.

"Is this still on your property?"

Joe pointed to a small iron stake on the far side of the rock ridge. "That's the corner of my lot, so I guess it is."

Joe knelt and examined the rock, saw streaks of quartz—pretty big ones—in the rock, and looked down the creek bed and saw where Hope had taken shovelfuls out. Two shovelfuls had been taken out upstream of the rock. Joe looked at Hope.

"Nothing from those," she answered the unspoken question.

Joe nodded, and they walked back. He took the sledgehammer and other tools out of the bed of his truck and set them on the front steps—away from where he and Hope would walk—and he and Hope went inside. Over fresh Pepsis, they talked.

Joe said, "Tomorrow's Saturday, so I'll be tied up there till late. But Sunday I'll—oh, hell."

"What's the matter?"

Joe grimaced. "I need to get gloves—heavy ones, two sets—and a pair of tongs, like a giant pair of pliers. You're going to have to hold the rods against the rock while I hammer the top of them, and you don't want to be holding a rod with your bare hands if I miss."

Hope stared and then nodded.

"Otherwise," continued Joe, "you pan away tomorrow, and Sunday we'll begin busting up that rock ridge."

Hope nodded again. She and Joe sipped their Pepsis until Joe decided to get an early start on Saturday and went to bed. This was a real bed, with sheets smelling of whatever perfume the manufacturers put in the laundry soap, and actual blankets. As he lay back on the pillows, real ones covered with pillow slips, Joe tried to think how long it had been ....

Despite Joe's ambition of making an early start the next morning, things were rushed as usual, and he drove away, eating a sticky bun with one hand while driving with the other. At the lab, Joe washed his hands in the sink and went to deal with business. As the day wore on and on, he was very glad he had eaten some sort of breakfast. By midafternoon, he was beginning to wilt. He managed to score a Pepsi and his last two candy bars, and then returned to face more unhappy—no, heartbroken—clients. He let them talk, nodding agreement, trying to be understanding and exude sympathy until he was able to make his standard points about putting the welfare of the children first. Two of his clients asked Joe if he had ever been betrayed by someone he had loved, and Joe said, "Yes." That was all, but it reinforced his status as an emotional, not just technical, expert, and his clients left, saddened but thoughtful.

The last of the day had segued into evening before Joe was able to call Hope.

"I had leftovers, Joe. I'm exhausted. How was your day?"

"If it wasn't the worst, it was in the running. I'll try to get those gloves and tools, and a burger. Any luck?"

"Bring that Mason jar, will you?"

Reaching into his desk drawer, Joe said, "I'll weigh it again and be on my way."

It was past ten when Joe finally got home. Hope had left the outside light on—*Considerate,* thought Joe; *at least I'm less likely to fall on my face*—but inside, he could see her on the couch.

She woke up when Joe came in, and asked, "Got the Mason jar?"

Joe held the jar up and headed to the bar-counter where they ate. He began eating while Hope produced two sheets of paper, each with a sizable heap of gold dust. "This was all I had to dry it on," she said.

"I need to get some dishes—something with a big surface area, like a shallow soup bowl."

Hope poured the two heaps into the Mason jar and then added the contents of the two scintillation vials.

Joe stared. "Damn, Hope, I can't even guess at how much that's gonna bring. Twenty, thirty, forty thousand? You must be about wiped out."

Hope said, "I found a good pocket. But you're right. I am."

Joe saw a pea-sized nugget, got a spoon, fished it out, and gave it to Hope. "Keepsake," he said once again. Hope smiled and put the nugget into an empty scintillation vial. Joe ate his burger and drank a Pepsi.

"When and where is this going to be cashed in?" Hope asked.

"Monday and maybe Tuesday are too busy. Let's say Wednesday, lunchtime. You drive in with this," he said, indicating the Mason jar. "I'll get a weight on it Tuesday evening so we have some idea of how much there is. Wednesday we take our checks to whatever bank we use."

Hope nodded and got up rather stiffly, and the two of them went to their separate beds.

That Sunday, Joe and Hope took the gloves and tongs out to the rock ridge. Joe had Hope hold the rod in place while he began to swing the sledge. As Joe guessed, he missed a few times, with no harm done, but he hammered away until several good-sized chunks of rock were broken off. He and Hope looked at them closely. Joe selected a different angle of attack and kept smashing at the rod. This time, several of the chunks had quartz veins, and in the veins were smaller veins of what was indeed gold.

Both were very excited. Joe put down his sledge, wiped his face, and inspected the rocks more thoroughly.

After a minute, he said, "Now I need to get a heavy steel plate to smash these rocks so we can pick up the bits of gold. If we were doing this commercially, we would blast, put the big rocks in a crusher, and reduce them to powder. Then we would do the equivalent of panning, only on a much bigger scale."

Hope nodded, but said, "Joe, it seems that panning is going to be more productive."

"Hope, I'm just trying to promote a buying break, for me at least."

"I'll go with you." And off they went.

Finding a steel plate small enough yet heavy enough for what they wanted to do took more than two hours, at which point they decided on an Italian place for lunch. That consumed well over an hour, causing Joe to comment, "We aren't going to get rich this way. Not that I'm complaining, mind."

"Today is just to explore, to see what needs to be done."

Joe nodded, saying, "Well rationalized."

Hope laughed, and they returned.

Despite losing most of the morning, they were able to break many chunks of rock off the mother lode. They put the quartz-bearing pieces together in a bucket and carried them back to the house. On closer inspection, they were able to pull gold threads and wires out of some of the pieces, and added them to the Mason jar. By now it was getting dark and Monday was approaching. They ate some microwave meals and went to bed as before.

On Monday it rained, and Hope stayed indoors, resting up from Sunday. Joe got more items from the grocery store, and he and Hope ate together, mostly in silence because both were still tired and very stiff. The next day, the pace eased and Joe brought another extra-large, thin-crust Supreme back to the house. Hope liked the Supreme, and once more they finished it all. Then they got into Joe's truck with the Mason jar and drove back to the lab. Joe set the jar on the balance and turned it on. The numbers flew past the dial in a very gratifying way. Joe began to feel excited.

"This is looking good," he commented.

Finally the balance stopped. Joe wrote the overall weight down subtracted the weight of the jar, and took the jar off the balance. Now it read zero grams, as it should have. Joe used the calculator next to the balance to get the weight of the gold in ounces, and then multiplied that number by the price, less the 20 percent the refiner would charge. He explained each step to Hope. The final total came to just under $68,000.

Joe turned to Hope, who was staring, mesmerized, at the calculator, and told her, "A little under thirty-four thousand for each of us."

"Wow."

They drove back, not saying a word. When they went into the house, Hope carefully set the Mason jar on the counter.

"This means I can pay off all my debts, including the back rent, and collect my severance pay and maybe the pension money I'm due," Hope said. "The landlord has been keeping my mail to make sure I pay him. Now I can. This feels good. Thank you, Joe."

"You may need a few days for some checks to clear and such."

Hope nodded and then replied, "But things are turning right for me at last."

Joe smiled, nodded and said, "Great. Bring the jar to the lab about noon and I'll show you where the place is."

At Bonanzas Unlimited, they had a pleasant surprise: the price of gold was up, so they would each pocket nearly $36,000.

Joe told the manager, nodding toward Hope, "Half and half."

The manager cut them each a check, and Hope and Joe left.

On the way back to Hope's car, Hope commented, "He didn't ask for any ID. Why not?"

"The only reason I can think of is that the owner likes to operate the way gold buyers did in the Old West, before the IRS. How he's able to get away with it is something I don't understand. Best just to cash the checks."

"Are they good?"

"Yes."

"When can I get money from my account?"

"Right away, in my experience."

Hope perked up at this. As it happened, they both used the same bank, but Hope had to clear up an overdraft her boyfriend had left. Joe just deposited his check. He waited until Hope appeared, carrying an envelope. She dropped Joe off, and Joe returned to work.

That afternoon Hope called. "Joe, I got my severance check and my contribution to the pension, so I'm feeling rich. Where do you want to eat? My treat."

Joe thought, then remembered the fancy Mexican restaurant his ex had patronized while Joe paid the bills.

"El Ranchero, but it's expensive."

"We'll go there. I'll make reservations."

"I should be home by six."

At El Ranchero, Joe and Hope sat in a booth. They both had dressed up a little. Hope wanted wine and ordered a bottle. It came first. The waiter opened the bottle and poured each of them a glass. They sipped their wine. Though no connoisseur, Joe thought it was very good. He inspected the label: California, but these days that was no disqualification. They sat, smiling at each other. Joe was thinking Hope wasn't bad looking, not at all, when he remembered Penny. He suddenly felt guilty.

"Joe, what's the matter?"

Joe evaded her question, saying, "I'm just not used to living this high on the enchilada. Years of self-denial have left their marks on my soul, at least the part that isn't mortgaged to some diabolical creature."

Hope laughed and raised her glass. Joe did the same, and they touched glasses.

"Maybe you can pay off the mortgage now."

Joe grinned in response.

Their orders smelled wonderful and tasted even better; the chili gravy was superb. Joe was impressed with his ex's taste; he was expecting to be impressed even more with the bill. He refilled Hope's glass, and his own. He was still feeling guilty but told himself he and Penny would be eating here, and often. But what about Hope? Joe tried to shake these thoughts off. He was helping a former colleague get back on her feet—that was all. Their bill arrived. Hope took an envelope out of her purse and left two hundred-dollar bills. Joe was very impressed indeed.

On Thursday afternoon, Joe got an e-mail from Penny:

> Joe, how are things going? Getting any gold panning in?

> My ex-boss needed a place to stay and something to do, preferably something that brings in money, so I invited her to stay with me and do some panning. I get half the proceeds but have had to do some work myself, I am very sorry to say. We have each pocketed over thirty-five big ones, and there is more to get. She is feeling a lot more cheerful.

> Is she pretty?

> Not nearly as pretty as you are.

> What is your new boss like?

> I am the new boss. A real son of a bitch, in other words

How is everyone taking the change?

They were very happy, the fools. Ha, ha, ha.

I think I had better sign off now—customers. See you Sunday.

Right.

Joe and Hope made fair progress, breaking up the rock ridge. Then, on Friday evening, a piece of quartz came loose, not with wires or veins of gold but a stalk. Hope pulled it loose and weighed it in her hand.

"This looks to be worth ten or fifteen grand."

Joe said, sweating, "Definitely worth the effort. It will have to stay separate; it won't go in the Mason jar."

"I suspect there is more where this came from."

Joe looked up at the sky and told Hope, "If there was a moon, we could continue. But I'm getting tired. Let's go back."

So they returned, linked by a feeling of common achievement.

WARNING SIGNS

On Sunday Joe tried to get up early to get the newspapers, but it was all uphill. He was feeling sore all over it seemed and worn out as well.

Eventually he got himself ready and left. He didn't tell Hope where he was going and felt guilty about it. She didn't say much, just ate and went out to pan. Joe bought sparkling wine and ten copies of the Sunday newspaper after making sure his and Penny's article was in the supplement. It looked fine, especially with the haunting image of the reconstructed face at the end.

Joe had a small burger for breakfast and then started for Winnemucca. He was a little early, so he took it easy. He even stopped to top off his gas tank near Lovelock. He got to the Echeverria ranch just about on the dot. Penny came out. There was also a guy, one of the ranch's shepherds, Joe guessed, hanging around. Penny did not look happy to see this guy but asked Joe rather formally, "Did you get the copies?"

Joe decided to play along, and held up the stack of supplements and the bottle.

Penny led the way into the house. Once in the office, things brightened. She had sandwiches and glasses waiting, and Joe handed her the stack and opened the sparkling wine. He poured two glasses. He and Penny touched glasses and sipped the bubbly as they called it, and then sat down and began looking at their article.

There were only one or two minor typos; the article looked good, read well, and had visual impact. Joe raised his glass once more to the image of the facial reconstruction. "Now everyone knows what you looked like," Joe said to the picture. "You're a human being, a man, not just 'remains.'"

Penny looked at Joe and nodded. They divided up the supplements—five each—and then sat back and finished the sandwiches and a second glass of wine.

Joe reached across the desk and took Penny's hand. She smiled at Joe. He asked, "When were you a student at Reno?"

"From 2005 to 2007. Were you on campus then?"

Joe shook his head, replying, "My ex had hijacked me to put her through med school."

"Why did you break up?"

"I discovered she was unfaithful and planned to dump me once I had paid off her loans." They were silent for a few moments before Joe resumed, "She didn't go quietly. I had to get a restraining order on her. I keep looking out for guys hanging around where I work."

"She sounds completely selfish."

Joe frowned and then said, "It seemed to go beyond that."

Silence followed. Joe was thinking that he and Penny might have gotten together if it hadn't been for Stacey.

He asked Penny, "Did you take the biology lab for nonmajors?"

"Yes."

"I was a TA in that class before going to work."

Penny stared at Joe for a moment before saying, "We would have met."

"Yeah."

Their eyes met. Joe was thinking how much happier his life would have been. He somehow got the impression she was thinking the same thing.

He was about to ask her about her ex when she said, "You had better head back, Joe. I can't discuss why right now, but Ramon, the guy who was hanging around, I don't trust him."

"Okay, Penny. We'll keep in touch."

"Yes, we will, Joe. But I need to get some things squared away here first."

They got up. Joe took both of Penny's hands in his, leaned forward, and kissed her. She put up one of her hands to touch Joe's cheek, and they kissed again as they embraced.

"Until we meet again, my princess."

"I shall count the days, my prince."

Then Joe left. Outside, he checked his truck. He always locked the doors, but he saw no problems with the tires, and the gas cap had a lock, too. So he got in and drove away, down the dirt road to the paved one leading south to Winnemucca. He recrossed the railroad tracks, drove through town, and turned onto the interstate. Once he had gotten to his usual eighty miles per hour, he more or less focused on the road, though his thoughts remained with Penny. Evidently there was something wrong, clearly something involving another man, most likely her ex.

Joe's attention was suddenly captured by a blue pickup in his rearview mirror. It looked like a Ford Ranger, maybe ten or so years old, coming up from behind. Partly out of paranoia, partly for the hell of it, Joe floored his accelerator. His truck surged ahead—it could outrun any Ranger, and Joe left his tailgate down whenever traveling on the interstate, which reduced wind drag. He pulled away from Blue Pickup.

They were coming up to an exit. There was a gas station on the road crossing I-80, and Joe decided to test his suspicions. He lit his right turn signals and pulled off to the right. Blue Pickup followed him, gaining. At the top of the bridge over I-80 there was a stop sign. Joe duly stopped, and then, since there was no traffic, pulled onto the entrance ramp on the other side. Blue Pickup went right through the stop sign. Joe again floored his accelerator, and was able to pull into a gap between two trucks.

Blue Pickup tried to catch Joe, actually driving on the shoulder, but Joe changed lanes, passing the truck in front. Blue Pickup had no chance, but the driver was clearly after him. The driver flashed the headlights, but Joe kept pulling away.

The chase continued. They were nearing Lovelock, and there was a knot of traffic ahead. Joe considered driving on the shoulder himself, but there was a bridge over the interstate up ahead. He pulled into the knot, had to slow, and saw Blue Pickup gaining on him. Then two or three cars in the knot pulled off I-80, for gas or maybe something to eat, and Joe was able to work through the cluster of cars and trucks remaining to come out onto empty road. Blue Pickup had gotten trapped. The driver once more tried to catch up by using the shoulder, but now there was a problem: a state trooper parked around a curve.

The trooper let Joe pass. Speeds of eighty or even ninety on a clear stretch of interstate were tolerated, but not what Blue Pickup was doing. The trooper lit up his car and pulled out ahead of Blue Pickup, then alongside, and Blue Pickup had to pull over. Joe continued on his way, grinning. His grin faded after ten miles or so when he had time to think about the situation. He would have to e-mail Penny and ask her about the owner of the blue pickup, though he thought he could guess.

Once in Carson City, Joe parked his truck in the parking garage and, after a very careful inspection of the surroundings, went to his office. He e-mailed Penny:

> Princess, someone in a blue Ford Ranger pickup was following me back, trying to get me to pull over. I outran the truck. Do you know who this is?
>
> Your Prince Charming (or at least Tolerable),
>
> Joe

Joe waited a few minutes without a reply, and left for home. There he found that the gas for the power generator was getting low. He loaded up his set of five-gallon gas cans and drove to the Speedy Fill. At the station he filled them and his truck's tank, which cost about a hundred dollars all told. At his house he backed the truck so the tailgate was over the front steps and began to haul the full gas cans onto the porch. Hope came out, saw Joe struggling with the cans, and picked up one of the pointed steel rods. She slid it through the handle of one of the gas cans. Joe understood what she was doing and grabbed the other end of the rod. Hope propped the front and screen doors open and took hold of the rod again. Together they carried the first gas can through the house, out the back door, and over to the generator. Joe poured the gas into the generator's tank. Joe and Hope moved the remaining cans in the same way.

Afterward, they sat down to have something to drink. Hope wanted just water, so Joe filled two glasses with ice and then water from the tap.

They drank in silence until Hope said, "This water tastes better than city water. Is it because of the chlorine?"

Joe frowned and answered, "Yeah, and also the pipe the city water is sent through."

Hope was thirsty. Joe refilled her glass and took more water himself.

"Joe, wouldn't it be easier to drive around the house and unload the gas cans there?"

Joe shook his head and replied, "The septic system—tank and lines—is on the creek side of the house. I don't want to risk driving over anything. On the other side of the house, the ground is too rocky. I would have to hire a bulldozer to clear a path, even if blasting didn't have to be done."

Hope nodded. A stray thought crossed Joe's mind: that it was comfortable sitting here just talking to Hope. There was more silence until Hope spoke again:

"Joe, I turned on the air conditioner. Is that okay?"

"Sure. I left it off because the house was empty most of the time. But you can make yourself comfortable. It does feel good in here with it on."

After their glasses were empty, they went out to have at the mother lode again. Joe was glad Hope hadn't asked where he had been. He wasn't sure why he felt guilty about being glad.

Joe hammered away at the ridge of rock and uncovered more gold veins. He and Hope pulled them out using tweezers where they could, and then Joe smashed the big quartz chunks with the sledge and heavy steel plate. They picked through the fragments until it got dark. Then they ate leftovers and went to bed.

Monday passed with no word from Penny, which worried Joe. He was thinking of sending another e-mail but got too busy, and after the day was done, he was too tired. He was also still stiff and sore, particularly his arms and upper back. Hope had asked for Chinese, and Joe, after a very careful look around, got the usual severalfold excess and brought it back. He also looked very carefully to see if anyone was following him but didn't see anyone. At home, Joe found that Hope had done some more panning and gotten more than half a scintillation vial's worth of dust. With the bits and the stalk, he figured they were gaining on twenty thousand apiece. Joe told Hope that, and she smiled.

On Tuesday afternoon, Penny finally replied:

> Joe, the guy driving the blue Ford Ranger pickup was my ex, who is very bad news. He got stopped by a state patrolman because of his driving, got into an argument with the patrolman, and is now in state custody. That is good, but he will be out again and will come looking for you. We have to talk. Come to the museum tomorrow if you can. Please. Penny

Joe checked around the office, figured tomorrow to be slow, and warned everyone he would be in late—maybe around two o'clock.

PENNY'S STORY

Joe left about eight o'clock the next morning and reached Winnemucca just after ten.

On the drive, his feelings vacillated between hope and fear. But as he got closer, he had to face the likelihood that he and Penny would be saying good-bye for the last time. Something, something in her life was very, very wrong. He went to Penny's office and knocked.

"Come in, Joe."

Inside, Joe could see Penny had been crying. He could also see scars on her face, scars Joe guessed she usually covered with makeup.

"This is my day off, so we won't be interrupted," she said.

Joe sat down. Penny wiped her eyes, blew her nose, and sat up in her chair. She leaned forward, and Joe did the same.

"My ex's name is Mack Foster. His dad owns a garage in town—fixes cars and pickups, things like that. Mack works there when he's not in jail. We dated in high school. Joe, you have to understand: Mack is very handsome, very smooth, and all the other girls in our class envied me. My folks didn't like him, and I think the feeling was mutual. Mack kept saying he thought they looked down on him, but I understand things differently now.

"Mack wanted to marry me right out of high school, but I wanted to go to college. The university offered me a scholarship, and I went. Mack wasn't happy at all. He started slapping me around, and then he apologized and was so sweet, I had to forgive him. In fact, he, well, he raped me—I think to get me to change my mind. But I told Mack I had accepted the scholarship and that I'd be able to teach school once I got my degree, so I could help out."

"After he raped you, I guess he was real apologetic again, right?"

Penny nodded. "Yeah. I've done some reading about spousal abuse, and Mack fit the pattern perfectly. Anyway, I went through three years at Reno, but Mack got me pregnant, and I had to drop out.

"You see, I am an 'only' because of that Rhesus factor thing, and I suspect Mack wanted to inherit our place. That's my guess. Anyway, my folks didn't want him living with them, so I had to stay in Mack's trailer. The stove didn't work, or the air conditioner, and the place was filthy. I think his dad lives in one too. I cleaned the place up, but it was damn hot, and Mack seemed to think I should be able to cook gourmet meals in a microwave that didn't work all the time. He started slapping me around again, then really hitting me and sending me to have my face put together again."

Penny pointed to the scars on her face, and Joe had to reach over the desk and take both her hands.

"Then my folks went to the sheriff, and he pulled Mack in and told him to stop or he would file criminal charges. Mack didn't like that at all, but he was apologetic again and tried to get me to promise I wouldn't testify against him. By now, though, I had had enough and told him to stop hitting me or I would file charges. Mack lost it then. He hit me in the belly, I miscarried—it would have been a boy—and the doctor told me I would never have another baby. And I did move out and file charges against him, and I filed for divorce too."

"Good," Joe said. "Good for you, Princess."

"Mack was convicted and given eighteen months. I think he served eight. When he came out, he came to me, swearing he was a changed man, that sort of thing, and asked me to please come back. When I said no, he told me he would kill me if I remarried and then kill my folks."

"Jesus Christ, Penny," Joe said. He had tears in his eyes too.

"Joe, I believed him and still do. When my folks and I were talking to the sheriff, he told us Mack's mother left his dad when Mack was ten. At least that is what I heard. But the sheriff said he wanted to search Mack's dad's place for his mother's remains because she just disappeared, and no one has heard from her or about her since. But he couldn't get a search warrant."

Joe stared and then said, "My God." It was all he could think to say. The hellish predicament Penny was in, the dreadful choice she had made and its consequences, still playing out, stunned him. He took her hands again. He had to say something, but what? If he and Penny married, they would both be looking over their shoulders for the rest of their lives. They'd have to buy guns for themselves and learn how to use them ....

"Joe, I got a court order to keep Mack from coming near me or communicating with me in any way, and the judge, the sheriff, and the deputies have been very good about protecting me. But if we married, I would have to leave my folks alone. I don't know if the cops where you live would be willing to spend a lot of time keeping Mack under control, and like I said, I can't have children."

Joe shook his head, but Penny went on. "Joe, if it weren't for Mack, I would marry you in a heartbeat. The only reason I was able to come to your dissertation defense was that Mack was in jail again. But getting to know you, working with you, has been so different, so much fun. I just wanted it to go on and on. But now that Mack has gotten wind of your existence, I can't see you again. I don't dare, for everyone's sake. I just can't stand the idea of anything happening to you or my folks. I just can't."

Joe felt himself, his hopes and dreams, falling apart. Penny must have seen how bleak the expression in his eyes had become because her own eyes filled again before she continued.

"Ramon, the guy who was hanging around on Sunday, is evidently one of Mack's drinking buddies, and he must have tipped Mack off about you. But my dad told Ramon he wouldn't tolerate disloyalty of that sort and fired him. So Ramon is on his way back to Spain. In case you were wondering."

Joe bowed his head. He knew what was coming and tried to steel himself.

"Mack may have more contacts among the men working for us. I don't know."

Joe clutched at the only straw he could think of. "Maybe another tour in jail will help."

But Penny shook her head and told Joe, "The really weird thing about his behavior is that he just gets madder at me, the more trouble he winds up in."

Joe stared at Penny; what she had said reminded Joe him of something ....

"Joe, we can't have any more contact—not e-mails or anything else. It has to be a clean break. Oh Joe, this breaks my heart too."

Penny was crying. Joe got up and held out his arms. Penny got up too and put her arms around Joe. Joe could hardly talk. He had to whisper, "Farewell then, my princess. May God keep and protect you and yours."

Penny swallowed and said, "So long, Joe, and may he keep you safe to find another love and, and be happy."

Here Penny began sobbing and Joe held her, comforting her until her sobs eased. Then Joe released her, and she released Joe. He stepped back, raised his hand in farewell, turned, and went out the door.

Joe got in his truck and headed back to work, to his home, which meant nothing to him now. For just the second time in his life, he knew what it was to want to murder someone. If Penny's ex had tried to catch Joe, Joe would have used the bigger weight and horsepower of his truck to run the bastard off the road, preferably into a gulley or a big rock. Three times he had to pull over to the side of the interstate; his eyes were so full of tears, he couldn't see well enough to drive. Joe's second quest for love had failed.

As he got closer to the turnoff in Reno, Joe realized that what Penny had said about her ex applied to Joe's ex, too. Both were totally selfish—no, no, the word was *controlling*—and when the people they were controlling broke free, the controllers went off the rails, blaming the people who had escaped for whatever bad happened to the once all-powerful controllers. Truly pathological behavior, Joe thought.

But what was it in Joe's and Penny's personalities that had caused them to become psychological captives of such people? Or was it just two doses of very bad luck? Maybe it didn't matter now. Anyway, Joe had to get back to work. People were depending on him. Once more, that was all he had now.

DISASTER

Joe pulled into the high-level security parking garage and parked in his usual slot. He got out and started walking to the GeneQuestion office. He felt so down, so bad, that he wasn't paying any attention to his surroundings. At an alley with some Dumpsters, he had to stop when a woman pointed a gun at him. Someone behind Joe grabbed his shirt collar, pulling him back into the alley.

Suddenly Joe recognized the woman: it was Stacey, now heavyset, with a mean expression on her face. For an instant, Joe wondered how he had ever imagined her to be attractive.

Then she said, "Get in the trunk of that car, Joe."

She was pointing to an old Chevy sitting in the alley with its trunk open. The person behind Joe stayed there, pushing Joe toward the car.

It was too much. Joe stopped, lowered his hands, and yelled, "No! No, God damn you to hell, you selfish, cheating bitch—"

"You ruined my life, you bastard," Stacey interrupted.

"You ruined your own life. If you had stayed faithful, had treated me with respect, we would—"

Joe felt a wind, then a heavy wallop to the side of his head. He was falling sideways ....

It was hot, so hot. Pitch dark. No air. Joe couldn't breathe, and the right side of his head hurt—hurt like hell. He tried to move but felt confined in every direction. He was in a metal box—not a coffin—and there was a strong smell of grease and rubber. Then Joe remembered: he was in the trunk of a car, the old Chevy he had seen in the alley. He was locked in, trapped .... Penny .... He had to try to get out. He felt for the trunk lock. Could it be opened from inside? He couldn't remember, had to try. But there was nothing, no catch, no lever.

Tools? He felt around. Nothing, no screwdriver or wrench or anything. He pushed against what had to be the seat side of the trunk—all metal, no give anywhere. He was sealed in; it might be years before his mummified body was discovered .... Penny ....

A light, a blinding light. Was this heaven? But someone had opened the trunk and was looking down at him. Joe began to breathe great gulps of air, the desert air of a Nevada summer; he was still alive.

Joe heard the man who had opened the trunk say, "There's a guy in here. Looks like he's hurt."

As Joe started to climb out, the man helped him. "Man, you got your head busted open. You're bleeding."

Joe reached up with his right hand, felt the side of his head. It and his neck were sticky with blood. He saw two men standing there. "How did you find this car?" he asked.

The two men looked at each other, and then one said, "We saw two cars go up this track. Coming back, we saw one of them going on south. We decided to take a look."

"I'm sure glad you did."

Joe was wavering on his feet now. He held on to the fender as he looked around. Things looked funny, not much depth in what he saw, but he could see that the car was on an overgrown track or trail between two hills. The hills had bigger trees and thicker undergrowth than the track the car that imprisoned him had, but Joe realized the car he had been trapped in had been driven up a path that no one else was likely to drive up on. It had been driven as far as it could go. Joe was not supposed to be found.

Then Joe noticed something else: he couldn't see out of his right eye. He rubbed it gently, but there wasn't a glimmer. That was very serious. He looked at the two men who had rescued him: unshaven; dirty, nondescript work uniforms; a tow truck behind them. Still, they were angels incarnate to Joe.

"I can't see out of my right eye. I've got to get to a hospital, fast. I'll need some sort of operation."

The two men stared at Joe. One of the men, the driver of the tow truck, Joe guessed, asked "What were you doing in the trunk?"

"Dying. My ex and some guy bashed my head in and threw me in there to die. Please, I need medical care ASAP."

Joe was beginning to shiver. Despite the heat of the day, he felt cold. He also felt sick to his stomach.

One of the men said, "Get in the front seat of the car and lie down. We'll take you to the emergency room and leave you there. Is this car yours?"

Joe, who was nearing collapse, said, "No. Keep it. And thanks."

The men helped Joe lie down in the front seat. He heard the engine of the tow truck start. The sound grew fainter and fainter. Joe started to panic, then realized the tow truck would have to turn around, which meant it would have to be driven to a more open space. Joe forced himself to be calm. Now that he could breathe, he took deep breaths. He heard the tow truck's engine getting louder. Joe wondered how the men had been able to open the trunk. Some sort of master key? A crowbar?

The tow truck stopped. Joe heard the truck door open, and then one of the two men opened the car door. The car had a stick shift, and the man checked to be sure it was in neutral. He closed the car door again. The tow truck pulled the car up onto the bed of the truck. Chains were attached, a lot of them. This seemed to take a long time. Then the tow truck started off.

Joe lay limply on the front seat of the car, on his left side. His head hurt like fire, and he could see out of only one eye. Still, he noticed a tire iron and a jack in the space in front of the seat. Despite his injuries, he could think, and immediately realized the implications: he was definitely supposed to die in that trunk. He feebly felt his pants pockets: no wallet, knife, or keys. His shirt pocket still held his ATM card; that must have been overlooked, though without the PIN, it would have been useless anyway.

In the front seat, Joe began to retch, over and over again. He hadn't eaten anything, and nothing was coming out, but that didn't help. In between spasms, Joe guessed the two men made their living cruising the highway, looking for disabled cars and just taking abandoned ones to a chop shop. But as long as they got him to a hospital, Joe didn't care. He left the driver's-side window down, though the hot desert air blowing over him would normally have been unbearable. Even so, he shivered and shivered.

The tow truck pulled up to a building. Joe heard the driver's buddy explaining. The car door opened. Two paramedics pulled Joe out and put him on a gurney. The tow truck left. Now Joe was in air-conditioning again. As soon as the gurney stopped, Joe asked for blankets. He also asked to see a cop. "I was mugged and robbed," he explained.

There was an officer on duty in the emergency room. He came over almost at once, while a voice over the PA was calling for the doctor on duty. Joe had just told the cop his name and where he was attacked when a young woman with a clipboard walked up.

"Excuse me, sir, do you have insurance?"

Joe retched again and then told the woman, "Yes, I work for GeneQuestion here. I'm the director. But the people who broke my skull and threw me into a car trunk to die took my wallet, which [another retch] has my KP insurance card."

The officer looked as though he were about to ask the woman

to let him finish his job when the doctor on duty appeared. He carefully looked at the side of Joe's head.

"I can't see out of my right eye now," Joe said.

The woman asked Joe, "What is your policy ID number, sir?"

"I can't remember a number that long with letters in it too. My name is Joe Stallings. You can look that up."

The doctor said, "Probably a blood clot on your brain. We'll have to do a CT scan and operate. I'll ask Dr. Peters—he's a neurosurgeon—to operate, but let's get you an MRI first."

The woman told Joe, "Sir, we can't use your name. Security!"

Now the cop stepped in: "Ma'am, let me finish talking to the victim. Mr. Stallings, did you recognize any of your attackers?"

"Officer, if you please, I need this information before this man can be admitted."

"There were two of them. One was behind me and the other was my ex-wife, Stacey Porter. She had a gun."

"She pointed it at you?"

"Sir, you can't be admitted ...."

"Yes. I"—he began retching again, this time in the direction of the woman, who quickly backed off—"don't have my cell phone or wallet. I think ...."

The gurney began to move, accompanied by the police officer, the woman, and two orderlies who were pushing the gurney.

The woman, keeping a safer distance from Joe, asked him, "Do you have any ID?"

Joe reached into his shirt pocket and found his ATM card. He guessed his attackers hadn't realized he kept the ATM card in that pocket, but then they would have had to torture him for his PIN .... Joe handed it to her.

Still keeping her distance, which made the cop smirk, she looked at the card and told Joe, "Sir, this isn't enough. There's no picture."

"It's all I've got right now."

They were about to go into the MRI room. Joe was able to

tell the cop, "They probably threw my cell and wallet into a Dumpster near where they attacked me—in the alley between the HiSecure parking deck and the GeneQuestion building. Here is my cell number." Joe wrote his cell number down on the cop's card.

"Call that number and listen for the answering buzz. The wallet may be findable, too."

The cop nodded and turned to leave.

The woman said, "Sir, I do need this information ...."

The door to the MRI room closed.

Joe was shivering again when he was set on the MRI table. He was strapped down and then advanced into the MRI, advanced twice, then twice more with his head turned sideways.

Now the neurosurgeon was there. He asked Joe about his symptoms, looked at the scans, and then came over to Joe.

"We'll have to operate, remove that blood clot, and put your skull together again."

The neurosurgeon turned to a nurse. "Have the side of his head shaved and prepare him for surgery."

An orderly or NA injected Joe's arm with something after his shirt was taken off, and Joe finally, blessedly, began to hurt less and less ....

ANGEL OF LIGHT

When Joe came to, he was lying propped up on a hospital bed, attached to a machine that monitored his breathing and pulse. He was alive, Joe was glad to see, and covered with two or three blankets. In fact, he felt hot. He hurt but not as much as before.

"Joe?" said a voice. It was Hope. She had been reading something, but saw Joe was awake. Joe suddenly realized he could see out of both eyes again.

He laughed and said, "I guess so. Dammit, Hope, I can see out of both my eyes again, so you are a sight for—you can guess. What day is it?"

Hope closed her book and told Joe, "Thursday about one a.m. It hasn't been that long. I called your cell, got no answer, called the lab, and was told you had gone somewhere yesterday morning, promising to be back by two, but hadn't shown up. So I started calling around and eventually was told that someone claiming to be Joe Stallings had been brought in, injured. I came over and ID'd you when you came out of the operating room, and I've been here since."

Joe reached out, and Hope took his hands.

"Joe, there is a cop outside who wants to talk to you when you wake up. Can you do that?"

"Yeah. Look, Hope, you are going to have to take over the shop again. Call HQ and tell them what happened. Use my office. And that means you need to get some sleep. Tell them you talked to me but I don't know when I'll be able to go back. You can do it, Hope. I know you can."

Hope seemed about to shake her head, but then nodded instead. "I'll bed down here in the hospital. Let me get the cop."

She went to the door, opened it, and said, "Officer, he's awake."

The plainclothes cop came in and looked Joe over. "How are you feeling? Can you answer some questions?"

"I'm feeling a lot better, and I'll try."

The cop sat down. "First, we found your cell and wallet. We got some prints off the wallet. No driver's license or credit card."

"Shit," said Joe.

"We did find your health insurance card, but we're still checking for prints on it."

"There's an extremely aggravating bitch from Admitting who wants to see that. I'll have to cancel my credit card right away. I'll be damned if I let those pieces of shit live high on my dime a minute longer."

"We want to track these people, and their use of your credit card is the only way we can do that," the officer said. "We want you to contact the credit card company, tell them what the situation is, and give us a few hours to nail them."

"Yeah, okay, I'll do it. I think my ATM card has the number. That should be in the drawer to my left."

The cop got up, opened the drawer, and, after rummaging through Joe's bloody, greasy clothes, found the card. He held up his cell phone to Joe. "Use this," he said.

Joe dialed the "lost or stolen" number. After many robodelays, a woman answered. Joe gave his name and explained the situation. The woman asked for the last four digits of Joe's Social Security number.

"Four three eight six. I work for GeneQuestion, if that's any help."

"When was your last purchase?"

"I got nearly a hundred bucks' worth of gas at a Speedy Fill last Sunday. Nothing since then."

"We show gas purchased in Las Vegas yesterday afternoon, then two meals at the Fontainebleau Hotel in Las Vegas. Whoever has your card booked a room there. There is a charge for a floor show last night and a significant cash withdrawal too. You are saying none of this is yours?"

"None. But let me turn you over to a police officer here."

Joe handed the phone to the cop. The cop identified himself as a detective and asked the woman to hold off cancelling the card for a couple of hours, until he had notified the Las Vegas police.

"The woman, at least, has a gun, so they must be considered armed and dangerous," the officer said. "They nearly killed Mr. Stallings here with a blow to the head, and then tried to finish the job by locking him in a car trunk, but I'll tell the Las Vegas police that. Just two hours, say, till morning, and we'll arrest them."

The cop listened for a moment and then said, "Fine. Will do," and ended the call.

The officer went on to tell his supervisors in Carson City about the situation, and finally dialed someone—evidently the Las Vegas police—and repeated his story. While this was going on, Joe looked over at the machine he was connected to, all blinking lights and oscilloscope displays, a little like a Christmas display. Joe noticed his temperature was a little high at 101.0 degrees, but his vitals seemed good.

A nurse came in and seemed about to object to the cop's presence, but Joe told her, "I'm okay. Let the officer do his job. It's important."

"You need rest, Mr. Stallings."

"And I'll get it once the detective here has finished."

"How does your head feel?"

Joe suddenly realized the pain in his head was getting stronger, so he replied, "The pain's getting worse."

The nurse injected something into a port on the line transmitting liquid from a plastic bag into Joe's arm. Then she recorded Joe's vitals and left.

The detective got up and told Joe, "The Lost Wages police will bust those two in a few minutes, once they ID them. You didn't see the guy?"

"No, he was behind me."

"We'll get 'em." He left Joe drifting, drifting ....

SOME LOOSE ENDS

The next morning Joe came awake. Now he was getting a little hot; too many blankets now. His temperature was down to 99.4 degrees, and his vitals looked about the same. Joe wondered how Hope was doing, and whether Stacey and what Joe guessed was her boyfriend had been arrested .... A nurse's aide came in with a tray: breakfast. She helped Joe sit more upright and then took away a second blanket at Joe's request. Joe began to eat. The meal was about what everyone said hospital food was like, but Joe hadn't eaten for .... since Tuesday evening, and it was now, yes, Thursday morning. So he finished the meal, lay back as he felt his head hurting more, and wondered if he should call the nurse.

The door opened, and the woman from Admitting came in carrying a clipboard. "Mr. Stallings, have the police found your insurance card yet?"

The nurse's aide came in too and took Joe's tray and left. Joe told the woman from Admitting, "Yes, but they're checking it for fingerprints."

She was not happy to hear this news.

The detective from last night, looking like he needed sleep, came in and told Joe, "Dr. Stallings, the police in Lost Wages arrested two people who were in possession of your credit card, driver's license, and Social Security card. They claimed to be Mr. and Mrs. Joseph Stallings but couldn't tell the police there what your middle initial stood for, and the man didn't look like you. His prints matched the ones on your wallet, and his real name is Bruschetti. He has a rap sheet for aggravated assault, and he's a suspect in a couple of disappearances."

"I can guess what his MO was in the disappearances," commented Joe.

The cop nodded and then continued, "There were two guns in their luggage, so we got Bruschetti on another charge. And your ex insisted we call her Stacey Stallings."

"Kinda strange," Joe said.

"Under that name, she's been working as a prostitute in a brothel near Lost Wages. We figure that's how she met this guy."

Joe was going to shake his head, but then he remembered and said instead, "What a comedown."

"Oh yeah, here's your health card."

He handed it to Joe. Joe checked the name and handed it to the woman from Admitting, who took it and left. Joe couldn't tell from her expression how she felt about getting her hands on it: relieved, still angry, what?

"We'll keep the wallet for the time being, but you don't need it right away."

"How am I supposed to tip for service in this place?"

The cop grinned and then continued, "We'll keep them separate, see if we can get one of them to turn state's evidence. We haven't told them you're alive: we're saving that. So they may think they are facing a Murder One."

The cop got up, nodded to Joe, and was on his way out when he turned and said, "We called Bank of America and gave them all this info. They said they'll stop payment on the charges Wednesday, but you need to call them to confirm that."

"I'll do that."

The cop left. The door opened again, and a man carrying a

stethoscope, who Joe guessed was the neurosurgeon that had operated on him, came in with a RN. The doctor looked under the bandages on Joe's head and asked him how he was feeling.

"My head hurts more, but not too bad, and I can see out of both eyes now. My appetite is back, and my temperature is returning to normal."

The doctor looked into both Joe's eyes with a penlight and then had Joe grasp the doctor's hands as hard as he could.

The doctor nodded, and told Joe, "Mr. Stallings, you are one tough son of a bitch. The whack you had on your head would have finished most folks, but I think we can probably let you leave in a couple of days. Do you have a family?"

"Just my parents, and they live near Detroit. Oh, and an older sister who's an MD. She lives in the same state, has two kids, but that's it."

"We will need to have you come in to have the dressings changed and eventually the stitches taken out. Any friends, acquaintances?"

"Yeah, there's a woman living in my house. Just lost her job, so she's looking for another. I think she'll be willing to drive me back and forth."

"Okay, we'll leave it at that. If there aren't any more problems, you can go home Saturday morning. Okay?"

"Sure."

The doctor left after saying a few words to the nurse. She produced a bottle of pills.

"One every four hours. No more often."

Joe nodded understanding, and the nurse poured a glass of water and gave Joe the first pill—a painkiller, no doubt, thought Joe.

He leaned back against the pillow, waiting for the drug to kick in. He decided he would ask Bank of America to disallow the bills run up by Stacey and what's-his-name. He would try to keep the old card. Right now the police had it, so there wouldn't be any more problems there. Would he have to ID

Stacey? If he did, he would. Testify against her? That, too. He had loved her so much .... He was getting drowsy, but his mind kept working. He wondered if Stacey knew about Bruschetti's possible connection to the previous disappearances, but guessed she didn't. Knowledge like that was dangerous as hell, come to think of it. If the police wanted to get Stacey to cooperate, to turn state's evidence, maybe they could scare her into thinking she was next on his hit list: she knew too much ....

Joe's eyes opened. Hope was there, and he grinned. She was clearly happy to see him again—happy for another reason, maybe.

Joe asked, "Okay, how did it go?"

Hope sat down and told Joe, "I think all right. Everyone was concerned about you, everyone wishes you a quick recovery—I don't think they're that happy to see me back, but I feel a lot better. HQ wanted to know how much longer you'll be here. I told them you were lucky to be alive, so all bets were off. They gave me a temporary contract, good until you can come back again."

Joe, after checking the time, took another pill. "I'll need someone to drive me here to have my dressings changed and the stitches taken out. Can you do that?"

Hope nodded.

"Hope, thinking about what happened, I'm sure there is someone in the lab or office who has been tipping my ex off about my comings and goings. She and her sidekick were waiting for me yesterday. Just something to keep in mind."

"Who would do that, Joe?"

"Stacey's been working as a prostitute in a brothel south of here, and I'm guessing that's where she recruits accomplices. So it's probably a guy, maybe unmarried, who goes to places like that. If I have to talk to her, I'll try to get that information out of her. I'm sure the police are working on her to get her to talk. The guy she was with is really the dregs."

The door opened, and the plainclothes detective came in, along with the woman from Admitting with Joe's insurance card.

She gave the card to Joe, who struggled with the urge to tell her to stick it "where the sun don't shine," but he knew he would need it again, so he put it in the drawer next to his bed with the rest of his things. She went out.

The cop grinned at the expression on Joe's face, nodded to Hope, and said, "Can you ID your ex? In a lineup, I mean."

Joe replied, "Yeah. I'm supposed to be sprung from this place sometime Saturday morning. Tell me, is she talking?"

The cop sat down in the other visitor's chair and said, "No, but she doesn't know you survived. She thinks all we have on her is being an accomplice to credit card fraud, being in possession of a stolen gun, that sort of stuff."

"How about I get to talk to her? The shock of seeing me may make her turn."

The cop nodded. "The guy is the one we really want to put away."

Joe was beginning to feel better, beginning to relax. "Come here Saturday morning to take me over to the station, and I'll do it."

The cop nodded and left. The door opened again, and a cart pushed by another nurse's aide came in. Dinner. She helped Joe sit up, set the tray in front of him, and left.

Joe looked at the meal, then at Hope, and said, "Care to join me?"

Hope looked over the tray and told him, "No, I wouldn't want to deprive you of a gourmet experience."

"I'm not sure of the relevance of that remark."

Hope laughed, and left Joe to his second meal at the hospital.

On Friday Joe had the bandages on his head changed. When she came in that afternoon, Hope said, "There's a cop on duty at your door, did you know that?"

"When you're famous, everyone wants a piece of ya. Maybe literally. Hope, maybe you had better ask .... No, never mind, that cat is out of the bag. Just as long as my ex doesn't hear before I talk to her. How was today?"

Hope looked worn out and depressed. Joe understood just how she felt. Instead of replying, she asked, "How are you feeling, Joe?"

"Maybe I'll recover from this after all. Don't know when they'll let me on my feet. I can see how your day went."

Hope shook her head and told Joe, "It just broke my heart, over and over, having to tell couples their child has some awful, untreatable genetic disease. And telling some guy that the woman he loved and trusted cheated on him—I don't know how you stood it."

Joe said sadly, "I was doing it for someone else."

Hope looked at Joe a moment and then went on, "I guess that was why I hid in my office. I was afraid of getting emotionally involved.... But everyone in the lab sends their regards and hopes for your recovery."

"Thank them for me and tell them the holiday will be over when I get back."

Hope laughed and said, "I'll do that." She sat down. "Joe, I thought adultery was mostly something men did."

"Statistically, that is probably still true, though less and less. It's all selfishness, but those are the times we live in. It's fashionable, so people do it."

Hope nodded and then asked Joe, "Are you still good for Saturday? Just give me a call and I'll take you home, customers or not."

Joe smiled. "We may have to have a cop on duty at the house until the trial is over, maybe longer—so panning will have to stop."

"A rest from that is okay. Believe me .... Joe, I need your computer password."

"Just *J* period, *P* period, Stallings, only backward. Of course, you understand what this means."

"Means?" asked Hope, confused.

"It means I will have to have you killed."

Hope laughed, got up, and told Joe, "Say good night, Joe."

Joe obediently returned, "Good night, Joe."

Still laughing, Hope left.

On Saturday morning Joe's dressings were changed again and he was discharged. He was to return on Monday. He was also given a few more pills. He put on his clothes, including the blood-soaked shirt and undershirt. The hospital staff insisted on wheeling him to the cop car, though Joe thought he could walk, and the cop car took him to the public safety complex. He walked into a room with a one-way mirror, and five women paraded on the far side. There were a few other people on Joe's side of the mirror. Two identified Stacey as the guest at the Fontainebleau, and Joe readily recognized Stacey, who was looking sad and frightened. Joe resisted the urge to feel sorry for her, preferring to remember her expression as she pointed a gun at him.

Then Joe was led to a room with two chairs facing each other across a table. Stacey was sitting in one of the chairs. Joe sat down in the other. Stacey stared at Joe: clearly she hadn't heard Joe was alive. Joe looked her right in the eye, until Stacey's gaze dropped.

She shook her head. "Joe, I'm sorry ..."

"Can the bullshit, Stacey."

Joe was going to go on, but everything he had figured on saying evaporated, and his feelings took over.

"I loved you so much." His voice was hoarse, and he cleared his throat. "I thought the world of you. I was ready to make any sacrifice, bear any burden for you, but all you could think of was yourself. I can't begin to describe how much you hurt me—even before this." Joe pointed to the bandages.

Stacey was beginning to cry. But now Joe remembered why he was here.

"Okay, I want a few answers from you, and for your own sake, they had better be honest ones. Get me?"

Stacey nodded, her head down.

"Someone where I work has been tipping you off about my movements. I'm figuring a guy, unmarried. No, no, he is married but didn't want his wife to know, right? You blackmailed him, right? Answer me, Stacey. Remember, it's for your own sake that you should level with me."

Stacey could only nod.

"What is his name, Stacey? Give me his name."

Stacey's voice was low. "His name is Darryl Thomas. He works in the lab. I told him I only wanted to talk to you about a divorce settlement. He bought the story; he didn't have a choice. That's how we knew when you would be coming back Wednesday. Joe, I've been pissed off at you for so long. I blamed you for everything. I understand—I really do understand that my feelings of anger have bounced back and hurt me. Carlo told me you would survive; we would just take some of your money. I bought his story because I wanted to believe that."

"What did that guy hit me with?"

Stacey bit her lip, bowed her head again, and then finally said, "His gun."

Joe was glad to hear that because it meant the tire iron or jack from the car wouldn't be needed as evidence, even if finding them was possible now.

Joe now moved in for the kill. He told Stacey, "You understand that Carlo, or whatever his name is, is a suspect in a couple of disappearances, right? How do you think he pulled off the disappearances?"

Stacey stared.

Joe leaned forward. "And what did you think was going to happen to you once he had maxed out my credit card? You knew too much. Stacey, you get a public defender and you offer to talk. Turn state's evidence. The cops want Carlo, if that is his name; they want him a lot more than they do you. This is your chance, your only chance, to avoid serious time in the slammer."

Stacey put her hand on her forehead, a gesture Joe remembered from years ago.

"So what's it going to be, Stacey? Or rather, who's going to take the bigger fall, him or you? Better make up your mind fast, before he moves first. You don't really want me testifying against you. Me, I don't care."

And Joe got up and left the room. Outside, the cops who were listening nodded to Joe, and then two of them went into the room.

A third asked Joe, "You going to kick this guy Darryl Thomas's ass?"

"Yeah."

Joe went to the restroom, used it, and called Hope.

"I've done all I can here," he said. "Come get me when you can get away."

"I'll be right over, Joe."

Joe felt drained and sat down in the entrance area. The plainclothes detective to whom Joe had talked earlier in the week came over.

"She said she wants to make a statement, and needs a public defender," the detective said. "So I think we are going to nail Carlo, nail him good."

"Fine," said Joe. He remembered he had to call Bank of America, and did so while he waited for Hope.

Hope left Joe at his place. Joe insisted on lying down on the couch, telling Hope he didn't want to risk getting bloodstains on the pillow slips. Despite that, she brought one of Joe's pillows down. Joe put it under his head and, agreed, "Yeah, this is better."

Joe looked at his watch, got up, and downed another painkiller. He lay down again. Hope covered him with a light blanket, hesitated, and then set out Joe's cell where he could reach it.

"Thanks, Hope," Joe said, and she went back to work. Joe lay in a mental twilight until Hope got back that evening.

On Monday, Joe got his bandages changed. There were no signs of infection. Hope drove Joe to and from the hospital. On the trip back, he asked her if she had been able to keep up with the work at GeneQuestion.

"Yes." They were silent for a minute, and then Hope asked,

"Joe, did you find out who tipped your ex off about your movements?"

"Yeah. Darryl Thomas. He's been screwing prostitutes—sorry, 'sex workers'—and he's married and my ex blackmailed him. When I'm better, I'm going to have a few words with that bastard. Sorry, Hope."

"Are you going to fire him?"

"No, just kick his ass around—sorry again—and tell him what I think of his behavior."

It was three more days before Joe felt like coming back. Hope drove him in, bandaged head and all. She went out to make the rounds and to send Thomas in to where Joe was sitting in his old office. Everyone had been overjoyed to see Joe again—joy diluted by concern over his bandaged head. Joe thought Darryl Thomas looked a little nervous.

Thomas came in, looking much more nervous. He sat down in the chair across from Joe's. "Joe, we were all worried—" he started.

Joe said coldly, "First, you call me Dr. Stallings. Clear?"

Thomas, startled, nodded.

"Second, I didn't ask you to sit. Stand up, God damn you."

Thomas stood up, looking frightened. Joe looked him in the eye, or tried to; then he ordered Thomas, "Look me in the eye." Thomas did.

Joe let the silence continue, and finally said, "My ex, Stacey, told me she blackmailed you into telling her about my movements. She and an accomplice knocked me out"—he pointed to the bandages on his head—"then locked me in the trunk of a car so I would die from the heat or lack of air or both. Not a fun way to die, I can tell you."

Thomas was starting to sweat. His lips opened and closed as he tried to think of something to say.

"She has agreed to turn state's evidence. I don't know if you will have to testify." Joe let this sink in before going on. "I do not want you talking about me or my movements to anyone, anyone outside this lab. Clear?"

Thomas nodded, then forced out, "Yes, Dr. Stallings."

"If anything else happens to me, the cops are going to want to talk to you because they have your name."

Joe looked hard at Thomas, who swallowed and nodded once more.

"So if any guy or gal you meet, in a bar or anywhere, wants to know about me, about where I am or will be, you just say you don't know. Then you tell me. Get me?"

Thomas nodded yet again. Joe was thinking about Penny's ex. He didn't want to have to worry about another stalker.

"I will not tolerate behavior like you have displayed. I won't. Do you understand what I am telling you? Answer me. If you don't, I will tell you again, louder."

Thomas spread his hands, a helpless gesture, and finally replied, "Yes, J— Dr. Stallings, I understand. Believe me ..."

Joe cut him off. "I am not going to fire your ass, though I can and maybe I should. But there is another problem with your behavior." Joe paused, gathering his strength, and said, "Every goddamn day I am faced with telling clients about how their trust has been betrayed by people who promised—no, vowed—to honor them. You have been selfish and irresponsible toward your wife. Screwing whores carries a risk of sexually transmitted diseases, and there are lots of those around. You make an appointment with your doctor, tell him or her what you've been doing, and get tested for whatever can be tested for. If you have caught something, you go to your wife, go down on your knees, tell her what you've done, and beg her to forgive you. If she loves you, she will, though her trust in you may not survive. I won't comment about your morals; you are old enough to know better."

Joe leaned forward. "Well?"

Thomas nodded and seemed to struggle for words before finally saying, "Yes, J— Dr. Stallings, I will. And, and, I really am sorry. For you, I mean. I never thought—"

Joe told his worker, "Remember: if I had died in that damned trunk, you would have been accessory to my murder. Now get out of here and go back to work."

Thomas left.

Hope came in, looked at Joe, and commented, "I think I had better take you home. There don't appear to be any survivors of that meeting."

Joe smiled, pushed himself up, and let Hope drive him home. On the drive, Hope asked, "Did you put the fear of God in him?"

"I put the fear of Joe Stallings into him. If there is any good in him, that will be enough."

He sat, thinking. He had mixed feelings about being a bully—no, The Boss. But now Joe realized that he was really, truly in charge.

About ten o'clock on Wednesday, Hope drove Joe to the hospital to have his bandages changed. Although it had been only a week since Joe had been ambushed and nearly killed, it seemed like much longer. Then she drove him to the shop so Joe could help if any help was needed. There were a few things: orders and two meetings with clients. Uniquely, one man was delighted to find that the child he had been paying for through a divorce settlement wasn't his. Joe thought the client was going to start dancing as he left. The other clients were a husband and wife whose child was very quiet and withdrawn—but GeneQuestion couldn't find any genetic reason for his behavior. Joe could only suggest blood tests for anything unusual, and otherwise just accepting the child for what he was, a quiet, withdrawn individual.

It was close to two when Joe figured he had had enough and went to find Hope. She was talking to some of the technicians to figure out what had to be ordered. Joe was happy to see everyone getting along. Hope excused herself and went with Joe to what was now both their offices to get Hope's purse. Joe heard one of the technicians talking to another.

"You think there is something going on between Joe and Hope?"

Joe and Hope went out into the Nevada sun and headed for Hope's car. She was parking in the director's space, since she was the temporary director. There were delivery trucks and a service van next to the door, parked with their engines very close to the building, so Joe and Hope had to walk between and around them, out into the parking lot along the row of trucks. They were close to Hope's car when Joe heard someone yell, "Stallings!"

Joe turned and saw a big, tall man, a man who should have been handsome except for the snarl on his face. He was carrying a big switchblade and heading for Joe.

Joe quickly moved away from Hope into the middle of the parking lot. He knew this was Mack, Penny's ex, and that he was planning to do things to Joe that Joe wouldn't like. Joe's attention was on Mack, but he could also see that Hope had her cell phone out, probably calling 911 and also recording the scene.

Joe knew he had to keep Mack's attention focused on him, so he said loudly, "This guy's named Mack Foster. He likes to beat up women."

Joe kept moving, trying to edge to his left, but Mack was moving right at Joe, switchblade extended. A slight breeze from behind Mack brought a strong smell of alcohol. Mack was really sauced up, a little unsteady on his feet, but not unsteady enough. Joe decided to switch tactics. He kept moving, kept trying to keep from being cornered.

"This piece of shit beat up his pregnant wife so she miscarried and lost his child. So you murdered your son, you bastard—"

Joe jumped aside as Mack stabbed at him. That was close, but Joe had to go on. "Come to think of it, your dad murdered your mom. What was that about? Did he make you help bury her?"

For a moment, Mack stopped, his face showing shock before he said, "It was an accident."

"You all hear that?" Joe said to the small crowd from the lab that was growing bigger by the second. "He claims it was an accident. Did she hit her head on something when your dad knocked her down?"

Mack's jaw dropped in shock, and he said, almost in a whisper, "Her head hit the corner of the countertop."

Then Mack lunged at Joe, who jumped back again, almost hitting someone's car while twisting away from the knife.

"Joe!" Hope screamed.

She ran up and grabbed at Mack's shoulder, but he elbowed her in the face, knocking her away and down.

Mack swung the blade at Joe, slashing Joe's middle. Joe felt it cut but couldn't tell how bad it was. He tried to move around Mack but couldn't. Mack was closing in, beyond rage. This was all .... Then someone flew into Mack from his right side, knocking him sideways onto the pavement. Joe jumped onto Mack's right hand, the one with the knife, as Mack and the other man struggled. Mack tried to roll over and get up, but Joe stomped on Mack's hand, stomped as hard as he could ....

Now cops were everywhere. He was suddenly aware of the sirens. Joe saw the flashing lights of their cars. The cops grabbed Joe's rescuer, then Mack.

"Not this guy," Joe said, pointing to someone in a lab coat. "He saved my life." It was Thomas, Darryl Thomas, the technician Joe had chewed out just a few days earlier.

Joe pointed to Mack, who was struggling with two officers who were trying to cuff him. "This guy was trying to murder me."

Joe pointed to the switchblade, and then back to Mack, who was being pulled to his feet, his hands cuffed.

"Let this one go," Joe ordered, and the cops did so, releasing Thomas.

Mack screamed at Joe, "You broke my hand, you ...." but the cops put him in a car and closed the door.

Joe was totally winded and his cut stomach was starting to hurt like hell. He bent over, his hands on his knees.

Thomas asked, "You all right, Dr. Stallings?"

Joe looked up at Thomas and said, "From now on, it's 'Joe.'"

He lightly punched Thomas's shoulder and grinned at him.

Thomas grinned back. Hope was there, obviously very upset, seeing the blood on Joe's shirt.

"Joe, there's an ambulance here. Can you walk?"

"Sure."

But a man and a woman with a gurney insisted that Joe lie down. Thomas bent over Joe. "Dr. Stallings— Joe, Joe," he said in a low voice. "I never talked to that guy. I've never seen him before, I swear."

Joe thought a moment as the attendants strapped him on the gurney and told Thomas, "I believe you. I think I know who did."

It had to be Ramon, Mack's drinking buddy from the Echeverria ranch.

The attendants were wheeling Joe toward the ambulance. Joe realized all the people from GeneQuestion were there, all taking pictures. "Back to work, people," he said. "Show's over. Or I'll take it out of your salaries."

Everyone laughed.

Joe looked up at Hope. "Get those loafers back to their grindstones."

Hope was crying. Joe raised his hand to wave reassuringly, but she took it in her hands and bent down to kiss him. Joe smiled encouragingly at her as he was pushed into the womb of the ambulance.

At the hospital, Joe refused a general anesthetic and asked for just a local. The slash was "superficial" Joe was told. Still, it was long enough and deep enough to require seventeen stitches. And the hospital insisted Joe stay overnight "for observation." Joe was really feeling the reaction now, and didn't argue. He lay in a mental twilight, coming back when the neurosurgeon that had operated on Joe's smashed head came in for a look.

"We can't seem to get rid of you," the surgeon said.

"Satisfied customers always come back."

The surgeon laughed, and told Joe the stitches in his scalp looked fine and could come out in another week. Joe nodded.

He dozed again, until he was interrupted by a plainclothes

cop. The nurse on duty wasn't sure Joe should be seeing visitors, but Joe waved the cop on in.

The detective sat down and asked, "How are you feeling?"

"Good enough to answer questions."

"This Mack Foster guy: you know him?"

"Only by reputation. He was married to a woman I was seeing. She divorced him for spousal abuse some years back. He's got a rap sheet. My guess is he was imagining I was keeping them from getting back together."

"Were you?"

"No way in hell she would ever go back to that bastard. But— and you need to tell the Humboldt County sheriff this—I heard him admit that his dad killed his mom. He was slapping her around, and her head hit the corner of a countertop. I think other people may have heard him say that too. I was told the sheriff wants to search the father's place for her remains. Nice pair."

The cop shook his head and then told Joe, "We found his vehicle ...."

Joe interrupted, "A blue Ford Ranger, about ten years old?"

"Yeah. It had a bunch of empty beer cans, and there was pot under the seat."

"Sauced and stoned," commented Joe.

The cop nodded, and went on, "We figure he was waiting for you to come out."

Joe shook his head and remarked, "If I had just stayed at work a few more hours ...."

The detective laughed, got up, and said, "Can you ID him in a lineup tomorrow?"

"If they spring me from this place. I'll give you folks a call."

The cop left. Joe began to relax again. Then a NA came in with dinner. Joe looked it over, but it didn't stir his appetite in the least. Hope came in. Joe looked up and grinned at her. She was still upset. He could see a bruise developing on her face.

"Aside from that, Mrs. Lincoln, how did you enjoy the play?"

Hope began to laugh, sat down, and told Joe, "We got

everything done. One of the sequencers is starting to act up, but I phoned in for repairs."

"Which one?"

"The old one."

"We need to get rid of that one and get a new one."

Hope nodded. She looked down at her hands a moment and then asked, "What's the verdict?"

"Superficial cut but seventeen stitches."

"Joe, who was that guy?"

Joe thought a moment and decided he had better level with Hope, although he wasn't sure why. But he told her.

"He's the ex-husband of a woman who works in the Museum in Winnemucca that I fell in love with. She wanted to marry me too, but he was threatening her and her folks if she ever remarried, and she believed him. Well, you saw him in action."

Hope nodded. Joe went on, "She was afraid to marry me, so she insisted we break up completely, with no further contact. Unfortunately the guy, Mack Foster, didn't know about that, or so I guess. So he came gunning for me."

"How did he know about you—I mean, who you are, where you worked, that sort of thing?"

"This woman and I wrote a piece that just appeared in the Sunday supplement that had my name and where I worked. And one of the people who worked for her folks was a drinking buddy of Foster's. He must have described me and my truck. All he had to do, once he got out of jail, where he spends a lot of time, was wait for me near the GeneQuestion building."

Joe was silent a while, but thought he had to continue: "You must have noticed the house isn't painted .... I was figuring that when I brought her there as my bride, she could have the place fixed up the way she wanted." Joe shrugged, and tried to smile at Hope. "So much for plans."

Looking at Hope, Joe could see sympathy, but there was something else, something he couldn't figure.

"But if this Foster character is going to be locked up, maybe you can get together again?"

Joe slowly shook his head and replied, "He'll be out again and madder at me than ever. That's the way he thinks. At least he didn't have a gun. This time."

"Why did you move away from me in the parking lot?"

Joe roused himself to answer. "I guess partly to get him away from you, so he wouldn't take you hostage. I saw you had your cell phone out. And I rode his ass to keep his attention on me—oh, I was just mad at that dirtbag. I wanted to tell him what I thought of him. Well, I did."

Hope was silent for a moment and then asked, "So why are they keeping you here?"

"I think the only reason I have to stay overnight is so KP will pay for a day's stay."

Hope nodded and got up. "I guess I'll get a Supreme for myself."

Joe stared at Hope, looked at the hospital dinner, and said fervently, "Damn."

Hope left, laughing at the expression on Joe's face.

DUMPSTER GAMES

Joe was getting ready to leave the office on a late January evening when the phone rang. It was Detective Ferguson. Because of Joe's frequent contacts with the local police over the years, they kept him up to date.

"Thought you would want to know: your ex just finished testifying against that boyfriend of hers on federal charges. Evidently she heard a lot of things she shouldn't have. But the boyfriend was convicted and is going to spend his golden years in a federal maximum security pen. She's testified against some others too and given helpful info. So she's going into the Federal Witness Protection Program. She came to me yesterday after the latest trial and asked me to give you a message. She said to tell you, 'I'm sorry, Joe.'"

"Is that all?"

"Yeah, that's it."

"Okay, then, thanks."

Joe sat at his desk a few minutes, thinking and remembering. If only .... But saying she was sorry was the first step. Maybe now she would put her life back together. Joe hoped so. He sighed and got up to leave.

It was past six and nearly dark, with a cold nasty wind. Joe came out of the GeneQuestion building after his usual look around from inside. He was walking past the alley where Stacey and Carlo had ambushed him less than two years before. There was still a line of Dumpsters along the near side of the alley.

Joe heard a car door open, then the clatter of an empty can on the street. He looked to his left and saw Mack Foster coming around the car. He had a gun in his hand, and he was coming after Joe.

Joe darted to his right, down the lane between the Dumpsters and the building. He heard Mack yell something and dived into the gap between the first two Dumpsters. He heard a shot, and something went by just as he was sheltered by the big metal boxes. Joe ran as fast as he could, crouched so Mack couldn't see him, out between the two Dumpsters nearest the street, then past the second, dodging into another gap. Another shot whipped by, and Joe could tell that Mack was coming down the alley after him.

Joe could hear Mack and could only hope Mack couldn't hear him. He turned to his right, running past the first Dumpster toward the street. Mack was moving into the alley on the far side of the Dumpster, and Joe hoped he would keep going farther into the alley.

But Mack stopped and yelled, "Stallings! My dad's dead. You killed him, you ——. Now I'm going to kill you, you ——."

Joe was breathing heavily; he opened his mouth so his breathing wouldn't make so much noise. Mack went into a gap between Dumpsters to see if Joe was between them and the building. Joe wasn't, so Mack began coming along the building back to the street. Crouching, Joe darted as quietly as he could along the alley side of the Dumpsters, past one, then a second, and then jumped between the second and third.

Mack was probably drunk, but he was fast on his feet, faster than Joe, and he must have seen Joe as he fired again. Joe heard something hit the side of the near Dumpster, so he turned to his left and dashed down the lane between the Dumpsters and the building again. Joe knew he needed to call 911 and tell the police what was going on, but that would tell Mack where Joe was and would take too much time ....

Mack was on the alley side of the third Dumpster, forcing Joe to take cover on the building side. Joe moved back toward the street, past the second Dumpster, and then into the gap between them. Mack was looking around the fourth and last Dumpster and began coming back along the building toward the street. At each gap, he looked back and ahead, trying to drive Joe somewhere so he could see him and kill him.

Joe crouched down even more, and ran as quickly and lightly as he could along the other side of the Dumpster Mack was next to, then into the gap. But Mack must have heard something because he was coming back up the lane between the Dumpsters and the building, so Joe jumped back into the alley and sprinted back toward the street. He couldn't go farther into the alley, as there were only four Dumpsters and then just open alley beyond.

Joe couldn't climb into the Dumpsters because their black plastic tops were down and opening the sliding metal doors would make too much noise .... but if Joe opened one and left it open .... Joe did that during one of his darts along the alley side of one of the Dumpsters. He hoped this would capture Mack's attention long enough for Joe to head back to the street, maybe get to the GeneQuestion building. No, that was too far away, maybe hide behind a car or a truck out in the street ....

Mack saw the opened sliding hatch, yelled something, and began shooting into the black plastic trash bags in the Dumpster. Now Joe was out of the alley, looking for a parked car, looking for someone to tell about what was happening, but there was only one car, it must have been Mack's, it was light colored and of foreign make, and Joe jumped around the hood, recovered his footing, saw the empty beer can that had caught his attention. He looked inside, the key was in the ignition, he tried the door, it opened, and Joe jumped inside just as Mack came around the nearest Dumpster. Joe started the car. It had an automatic shift and Joe had it in first gear He had just remembered to take the brake off when he saw Mack standing in front of the Dumpster with his gun. He was coming at Joe, but Joe turned the wheel and ducked down behind the dashboard as Mack began shooting at the car. The front windshield splintered and starred, but Joe managed to see well enough to turn the car at Mack and hit the accelerator as hard as he could.

The car hit something, then roared into the alley, and hit a Dumpster, pinning Mack between the car and the Dumpster. Joe heard Mack scream, a dying scream, and then there was silence. Mack was lying on the hood. Joe could see his face. Joe saw agony there, then nothing.

Joe turned off the engine. Then and only then, the police arrived—the police and dozens of cars and hundreds of people. Joe hoped no one had been hit by Mack's bullets. He opened the driver's-side door and got out. He could hardly stand.

A police officer came up and asked Joe, "This your car?"

Joe shook his head and pointed to Mack, who lay on the hood, the gun still in his hand.

"He was chasing me, shooting at me. I dodged him, got into his car, and hit him with it. In self-defense."

Joe pointed to the bullet holes in the windshield. The cop looked into the car, and at that moment, Joe smelled beer and piss. There was about a six-pack's worth of empty cans on the passenger side.

"You been drinking?" the cop asked.

Joe again shook his head.

The cop pointed to Mack. "You know this guy?"

"Yeah. He's a psycho. I don't know how he got out of jail. He got eight years for attacking me with a switchblade. Has a crazy grudge against me."

One of the cops wanted to cuff Joe and take him in, but another recognized him. "Dr. Stallings, what the hell happened?"

Joe finally was able to gather his wits enough to tell the cops,

"This guy is named Mack Foster. He was trying to kill me. I dodged him and killed him with his own car. Like I said before, it was self-defense. I need to sit down somewhere."

Half an hour later, Joe was able to give the police a statement, at least as much as he could remember. Thinking about it after he had told the cops what had happened, Joe could honestly say that killing Mack with his own car had been lawful, even public spirited, since Mack was shooting into a public street at Joe. Also, Mack would have continued shooting at Joe if Joe had tried to drive away in Mack's car. And even if the cops had arrested Mack again, he would have been out someday. But Joe knew in his soul that the real reason he had driven Mack's car into Mack was that Joe had had enough. He had wanted to kill Mack any way he could, and using Mack's own car had been the only way available to him. Mack had gotten Joe to commit murder. Joe didn't like to think about that, but he knew he would, maybe a lot.

Still, none of it seemed real. He got a Coke out of a vending machine and sat slumped, drinking it while the cops and medical people filled in the gaps. Mack was indeed dead, of massive internal injuries. He had also just gotten out on parole.

Joe asked the detective, "How? He got eight years."

The detective shrugged. "Good behavior."

Joe rolled his eyes. "In other words, he conned the parole board."

The detective nodded.

Joe said bitterly, "Well, he's good at conning people—for a while." He was thinking of Penny.

The detective said, "This guy's dad died in prison a couple of months ago. Cancer."

"In for killing his wife?"

"Yeah, what a family."

Joe thought a little and then told the detective, "That must have set Mack off again. He was yelling at me that I had killed his dad and he was going to kill me."

The detective nodded.

Joe asked, "Where'd he get the car?"

"He stole it. The owner left the key in the ignition, engine running, while she ducked into a gas station for something—'only for a few seconds,' she told us. Foster drove off with it."

"Ironic," commented Joe. "Where did he get the gun?"

"There are break-ins at gun stores all the time. We don't know where the one he was using came from. He also had four extra magazines and had emptied two. It was lucky no one else was hurt."

Joe agreed. He finished his Coke. He just wanted to go home, even though he knew he might be having nightmares for months, maybe the rest of his life. That and his guilt feelings were Mack's revenge.

The detective asked Joe, "You okay to drive back home?"

Joe shook his head, reached for his cell phone, and replied, "I better not. I'll call my wife."

CHRISTMASTIME

Joe looked at his desk and then checked his computer screen. All clear. His cell phone rang.

"Hello, Mrs. Santa," he said.

The voice on the other end asked, "Are you finished?"

"Yeah, just now. How about you?"

"I got my grades in, picked up the twins from kindergarten, and we drove around, looking at decorations. After that, we did some Christmas shopping, and I got a carry-out meal."

"What did you get?"

"I'm keeping it a surprise."

"I'm intrigued and on my way," said Joe, and he ended the call.

Walking to where his truck was parked, Joe passed the line of Dumpsters in the alley. But he really didn't feel much. His life was cushioned, stabilized now by his family.

Joe was home in half an hour, despite Christmas traffic, still moving well even through two to three inches of fresh snow. Inside, it was warm: the big Franklin stove in the living room was radiating heat, and the ceiling fans were turning gently, pushing the heated air back down. In the corner was a Christmas tree, a Douglas fir, its smell reminding Joe of many Christmases. The colored lights on the tree were winking on and off. The pile of brightly colored wrapped Christmas presents at the base of the tree was much higher than it had been when he'd left that morning. Joe took off his coat, kissed his wife, and then sat down in his chair. The meal was from El Ranchero, and Joe, his wife, and their two kids were ready to pile in.

As Joe ate, he marveled at how good the meal was, how good his life had turned out to be—finally. His daughter wanted half a tamale, and Joe served it to her. She looked at Joe with her mother's large gray eyes and smiled. Joe smiled back. Their son had Joe's watery blue eyes. He was well into a taco.

Joe looked at his wife, her gold necklace with the pea-sized nugget gleaming in the light, and reached over, taking her hand. Joe and his wife looked in each other's eyes and smiled.

Printed in the United States
By Bookmasters